EVA AND VALENTINE'S RETURN

Malcolm J. Brooks

authorHOUSE®

AuthorHouse™ UK Ltd.
1663 Liberty Drive
Bloomington, IN 47403 USA
www.authorhouse.co.uk
Phone: 0800.197.4150

Published by AuthorHouse   09/12/2013

ISBN: 978-1-4918-7716-6 (sc)
ISBN: 978-1-4918-7717-3 (e)

Dedication

This book is dedicated to Charlotte and Jacob.
May their lives be full of love and happiness

Thanks

My very special thanks go to Barbara, Carol, Margaret
A, Margaret B and Tracey for all their hard work and
for keeping me accurate on the birth of children and
oak trees!

Back to the past

Not many tales start in such a bizarre manner. I can only describe my circumstances as accurately as possible for you to understand the predicament I found myself in. Attached to my right wrist by handcuffs was a very pretty, twenty-something woman dressed in a policewoman's outfit.

OK, maybe any stag-do might end like this, but I was nearly sixty and to my knowledge was not expecting to get married in the near future. From what I could remember, I was already married and had been for some time. What's more, the policewoman was crying, no, bawling her eyes out, at what she could see.

Holding my left hand was a young girl I recognised. I knew her to be twelve years old. She wasn't crying, in fact quite the opposite, she had a beaming smile on her face from ear to proverbial ear. To make matters worse, in her left arm she held a child of about two years of age. For all that had gone before, it was not difficult to remember that the child was called Valentine; a strange name for the year 2008.

As I looked around at our surroundings it was clearly not 2008, and it was these surroundings that were making the lady to my right sob her heart out.

"Where are we?" she cried, "and who is that horrible-looking man?" She was pointing with her free hand at one of the most gruesome-looking gentlemen you would ever wish to see. I recognised him and knew why he looked so gruesome. He gave a toothless grin and I smiled back. I removed my hand from the young girl's, knowing that it would make the man disappear.

"Where has he gone?" she exclaimed.
This was not the time to explain but I would attempt to do so later. For now we had to take stock of where we were and probably more importantly, when we were!

Some of the details of what had happened to us began to return to my confused mind. I had been standing in the dock at the Crown Court in the city of York and had just been charged and convicted of kidnapping two young children. One was called Eva and I knew her well. Her parents were present in the court and, despite Eva's protestations of my innocence, they thought that I was the lowest of the low. If her rugby-playing Dad could have got his hands on me, my present situation would seem like a picnic compared with what he would have done to me.

Eva had tried to explain the strange story of how we had been on a mission of mercy to bring a father and son from the 17th century together for the first time. The story was incredible and was believed by nobody despite being close to the truth. The jury certainly didn't believe it and a long custodial sentence was coming my way.

The baby was a mystery to everyone else except Eva and me. His name was Valentine Walton and indeed he was born in the 17th century. In the mission that nobody believed, Eva and I had indeed reunited father and son.

The rest of what had happened was still confused, but I remember Eva, child in arms, clambering up the steps to the dock in which I stood and running straight into me, grabbing my hand as she did so. The result of what she did had produced the predicament that the four, no five, of us were in at the present moment.

I tried my best to calm the hysterical policewoman.
"It's OK. Everything is going to be alright."
"Where on earth are we?"
"I am not sure, but the old guy you saw will be able to tell us when he gets back."

Eva smiled as both she and I knew that Henry, for that was what he was called, had not gone anywhere. He was still there but only Eva could see him. She had magical powers which allowed her to see both the living and the dead. Anybody in contact with her had the same powers, as the young policewoman had found out to her horror.

"Why did he look so horrible, with all that blood?" she sobbed, her hysteria beginning to subside.
Eva and I looked at each other, neither of us wanting to tell her the truth, 'because he's dead!'
"He's had an accident." Eva was being economical with the truth.
"Where is the Crown Court? This is not York is it?"
It might have been, but not as she knew it.

"Do you know where we are Eva or what time it is?" I tried to ask as unemotionally as I could.
"Henry says we are in London, his birthplace."
"And the time?"
There was a moment's hesitation whilst, I assume, Henry told Eva the year of his birth.
"1605."
"It's turned four o'clock?" the policewoman exclaimed, "but it was only eleven o'clock when the verdict was announced!"

"Look, I'm sorry about this, but I don't know your name."
"PC Collin," came the formal reply.
"No, your first name."
She hesitated before giving this very informal piece of information.
"It's Grace, Grace Collin."

"O.K. Grace, we need to explain some very difficult things to you. Some may seem unbelievable to you but they are the reason I was in court in the first place."

"You're not trying to tell me that you are innocent of kidnapping those two poor children?"

"You mean those two children?" I said, pointing to the smiling Eva and the now giggling Valentine. "I believe that you have also been responsible for stealing those two and bringing them here when they should be with their parents."

The poor girl looked confused.

"I haven't kidnapped anybody."

"Well, how come they are here in this place with you and not in court with the judge and their parents?"

I was being cruel and Eva knew it.

"John is innocent, PC Collin," Eva said politely "it was me that got him into trouble in the first place and now I have got you both into trouble."

Grace looked perplexed and I couldn't blame her.

"You must listen carefully and try your best to understand what is being said."

I recounted as best I could, with a few interruptions from Eva, the outline of how we reunited little Valentine with his father; the slightly larger but dead Valentine. I left Eva to demonstrate once more the magical powers she possessed, which, I am afraid, caused PC Collin more distress and more teary outbursts.

In order to do this, Eva again took my hand and, since I was still in enforced contact with PC Collin,

5

this allowed Eva to introduce her to Henry Pickering. Henry had helped us in our mission of mercy during the Civil War but he was not a pretty sight as he had been murdered whilst riding his horse near Doncaster in 1642!

Anyway, I digress. Eva's powers were in the main, two fold. She could see ghosts like Henry and when Eva touched other people so could they, hence the introductions that were now being made.

Her second magical power, and the one that got me into the mess I was in, was to be able to walk down 'corridors of transit'. I won't bore the reader with the exact detail at this moment. Suffice it to say that Eva, and anyone that she was in contact with, could walk down a tunnel to a ghost's birth place and time. In order to do this she must walk straight through them (the ghost that is!) and down what I had experienced to be a bright corridor which provided the link into the past.

During the last few minutes of explanation to the young policewoman, it had dawned on me what had happened in the court room in York. Eva, with Valentine in her arms, had grabbed me, and since I was at that moment handcuffed to the unfortunate PC Collin, she had dragged us both towards Henry. Unknown to me, he must have been stood behind us, ready for Eva to pull us down his 'corridor of transit' back to 1605, which presumably was his year of birth.

I am not sure that all this made sense to me (and clearly it did not to PC Collin) but we were now in the predicament of not knowing where we were or the exact month we were in. Only Henry had the answer to these questions!

"You mean that we are in the year 1605?" stammered Grace.
"Yes, that was when Henry Pickering was born. Look behind you."

Eva touched me on the shoulder and tossed her head, motioning for me to look in that direction. I could see that Henry looked sad at the scene that was before him. I half expected him to ask Eva to touch his mother so that she could see him now, but that wouldn't have been a good idea. His young mother would not have wanted to see Henry in the condition in which he died.

The room was quite dark with the only illumination coming from a few small candles.
But there, dressed in rags was a young woman, who had just given birth and the little bundle that she held in her arms was dear old Henry.

She looked tired, as you might expect, and maybe just a little alarmed at the sudden appearance of four people. Fortunately for her, she was not able to see the fifth member of our party and therefore she could not see how unattractive her lovely son had become!

As suddenly as Henry and his mother had appeared they disappeared as Eva let go of my shoulder.

"Who is she?" asked Grace, clearly not quite yet understanding the situation.

"It's Henry's mother," said Eva "and the baby is Henry. Henry has brought us down his 'corridor of transit' to the place he was born and at the time of his birth."

"We need to leave here before we are discovered in these clothes and arrested."

"Why should we be arrested," said Grace.

"Because we are different," said Eva "and they are suspicious of people who look different."

"Who are?"

"People who live in this time, in the 17th century. Say 'goodbye' to Henry. He can't leave this room unless he returns to York in 2008."

"He can take us back to the court room?" said Grace, with a note of relief in her voice.

"Well, he could do, but he's not going to," said Eva firmly.

"Why not?"

"Because we have a job to do while we are here."

"What job?"

"To return Valentine to his mother, Hester."

Eva had that 'I'm not to be messed with' look in her eye and although Grace didn't know it for certain, there was no way we could go back without Eva's powers. So what Eva said went and no policewoman was going to change her mind.

"What are we going to do then?" I enquired.

"Well, Henry says that he can get some clothes which will make us less noticeable."

"How can he do that?" I asked.

Eva listened to Henry's answer and said, "Never you mind!"

Not a lot I could say to that!

"Where exactly are we once we step out of this house?"

Again, there was a pause as the answer was relayed through Eva.

"In London, just off the Strand. That's on a Monopoly board isn't it?"

"Yes, next to Trafalgar Square I think. But I don't think Trafalgar Square has been built yet!"

"Why not?"

Grace beat me to the answer. "Because the Battle of Trafalgar hasn't been fought yet!"

At least she seemed to be understanding the situation that she was in a little more clearly.

We waited a few minutes for Henry's return. From where we didn't know, but suddenly it started to rain clothes!

"Henry, we do have another problem," I said, holding up my right arm and of course Grace's left. Although I couldn't see him, I assumed that he was back in the room and could hear me.

"Henry says that that could be tricky!" said Eva, although I felt that Henry wouldn't have put it quite like that.

"No it isn't," said Grace "I have the key attached to my belt."

She unhooked the keys and proceeded to unfasten the handcuffs.

"If my sergeant ever finds out that I let you go, I will be in big trouble."

"Trust me, I am about to run nowhere."

We took some time to sort out whose clothes were whose. In fact, Henry hadn't done a bad job size wise, but the clothes were obviously second hand and well-worn.

Although now wasn't quite the time for modesty, each of us did move into a darker area to put on these 17th century clothes over our 21st century underwear; quite a combination.

"What shall we do with our other clothes? We will need them for when we get back." Eva said optimistically.

OK. So what could you do with a brand new suit I had bought for the trial, a girl's dress and cardigan, and a policewoman's uniform?

We decided that we would leave them here in Henry's house and maybe come back for them if needed.

"Is Henry still around?" I asked Eva.

"Yes."

"OK, Henry we know it is 1605 but what date is it?" I said, knowing that I would not be able to hear the answer. At least I had not done what I had done numerous times before and asked Eva to ask him. He could hear me, but the problem was I could not see or hear him. The answer could only come back to me via my interpreter, Eva.

"What did he say?" I said impatiently.
"The twentieth of March! Oh no, it's happened again."

I knew what she was complaining about. Once before we had descended a 'corridor of transit' only to find that the date we had moved to was after the eleventh of March, which was Eva's birthday. The trial in York had been taking place in the middle of February but in using Henry's corridor to his date of birth we had moved onto the twentieth of March, so again missing poor Eva's birthday.

"I've missed my eleventh and thirteenth birthday parties!"
"Don't blame me. You got us all into this mess!"

Eva smiled. In her mind these adventures beat any birthday party. Grace looked perplexed but did not say anything.

"What time is it Henry?" Eva beat me to the next question.
"It's about six in the evening." Eva seemed to answer her own question but of course had been prompted by the invisible Henry, well, invisible to Grace and me that is.

"Is there anywhere we can stay for a while, Henry? We need time to think of what to do next."
Henry must have answered Eva's question and she was satisfied with the answer.

"What did he say?"

"The Duck and Drake Inn, which isn't far away. Henry has given me directions."

Her tone of voice meant, 'don't either of you two adults ask me to tell you the directions, I can remember them on my own!'

I took Valentine from Eva's arms and the four of us made our way to the door through which none of us had entered.

Before we opened the door to enter the street Eva said, "Look what I brought." She unhooked a rucksack from her back, which up to that point I hadn't even noticed was attached to her.

From the rucksack she produced a supermarket plastic bag which contained several items. "You remember you went to the supermarket before our last trip, John? Well, I did the same. Look!"

In the dim light I could see various items. "Where's the torch?"

"Here!" she said "and I've got spare batteries."

This was a reference to a mistake I had made on our first trip into the 17th century and she gave me one of her knowing smiles.

Nervously I opened the door onto the street.

The Duck and Drake Inn

We located the Duck and Drake Inn without too much of a problem. Eva had remembered Henry's instructions pretty well. We didn't seem to attract too much attention dressed as we were, although I noticed Grace got a few admiring glances from some of the better dressed men that we passed.

To say that the inside of the inn stank was a bit of an understatement, and we did get some disapproving looks, presumably because of the two young children that accompanied us. In the dimly-lit main area you could make out lots of tables and, although relatively early in the evening, there were quite a few people having a relaxing drink of something or other.

We made our way to the darkest corner of the room and took the table next to a group of men who seemed not to be drinking too much but were in deep conversation about something of importance.

The one doing most of the talking looked up for a moment and then resumed his speech to the rest of his captivated audience.

"I'll go and find the landlord and see if they have any rooms."
"But you haven't got any money from 1605 have you?"

Grace had a very good point and I was just about to return to my seat when Eva said, "Here you are, John." She gave me a number of strange looking coins.
"These aren't the ones from our last trip are they, because they might have the wrong king's head on them? It's not Charles who's king now. It's James I think.
"Henry gave me them so they should be alright."

I looked at the coins and to my surprise they didn't have a king's head on them at all but the head of a queen! It was Queen Elizabeth but not the one with which we were familiar.

I hadn't a clue how much they were worth or how long a stay at the Duck and Drake they would afford us, but with a degree of nervousness I made my way to find the landlord. I had only walked a short distance when I noticed that one of the party of men from the table opposite had left his seat and was now talking to Grace. Maybe they hadn't liked a group of people moving within earshot of what they had been so earnestly discussing.

Out of protective curiosity, I turned around and walked back to the table.

The man was tall, well-built and I would guess, in his early forties. He was well-dressed with his cloak, jacket and shirt buttoned up to a high collar. He didn't seem the type of man who would address a thirteen year-old girl, so I assumed that he was talking to Grace. However, as I neared the table it was Eva who, predictably, was speaking.

"We are taking Valentine back to his parents," Eva was explaining, hopefully not in too much detail about our circumstances.

"Can I help you, sir?" I enquired, trying to be as formal as I could.

As he turned to face me I could see that he had quite a skin disorder, a form of eczema I assumed, as his face and hands were blotchy. I raised my estimation of his age as I could now clearly see greying hair. He seemed annoyed at my intervention.

"This is John, my father," lied Grace.
His demeanour changed slightly.
"I am very pleased to meet the father of such a beautiful young lady. I am Thomas Percy, a descendent of the fourth Earl of Northumberland."

I suppose that was to impress me as it became obvious that the target of his approach to our table was Grace.
The "I'm his daughter too," from Eva fell on stony ground as far as Thomas was concerned and Eva looked a bit miffed.

Grace continued the story that Eva had started. "We were just explaining to Mr Percy our predicament regarding somewhere to stay before going to meet Valentine's parents."

"Why don't you all come and stay with me. I have a large house with many bedrooms not far from here." Grace shot me a glance which clearly showed worry and concern about such a suggestion.

"YES PLEASE!" exploded Eva, "That would be great, sir," The 'sir' came a few seconds after the rest of the statement as Eva realised that politeness was needed after such enthusiasm.

"That's agreed then! I have just got to finish my meeting with these gentlemen and then we will away." He turned and resumed his seat at the table where the other men were still deep in conversation.

Once out of ear-shot, both Grace and I tried to explain why staying with Mr Percy might be a bad idea.
"We don't know what he is like!" exclaimed Grace, "he might be a criminal."
"Why do you police always think the worst of people? He might be a nice person trying to help us!"
Grace realised that it was no use arguing with Eva.
"We must just be careful, that's all."

"Wasn't it the Earls of Northumberland who owned Alnwick Castle?" Grace asked.
"Yes they did."

". . . and parts of the Harry Potter films were done at Alnwick Castle!" Eva joined in.

"Yes you are right," smiled Grace as she was coming to terms with the fact that this was not just any old typical thirteen-year-old girl.

The house at Westminster

Whilst we were discussing whether or not to take up Thomas Percy's offer, someone, who looked like he was a clergyman, approached the table where the meeting was taking place. Shortly afterwards, the meeting broke up and Thomas came over to inform us that they were going to have a further meeting in another room and that they would return in about half an hour.

Since there was not a better option we decided that we would stay, for a short time at least, at the house of Thomas Percy. It would give us time to consider our options and select the best course of action.

Thomas was true to his word and the men re-appeared around thirty minutes later.

"If you would care to follow me, my house is not too far away. It's in Westminster."

On the short walk to the house it was clear that our Mr Percy was very interested in Grace. For whilst they walked side by side, deep in conversation, Eva and I, with Valentine in my arms, walked behind them with a very quiet, almost sullen man who Thomas had said was one of his servants. The man, who had also been at the meeting, had been introduced to us as John Johnson. Although that seemed a very English name, from the few words that he uttered he was anything but English.

His manner too didn't seem as deferential as one might expect from a person of such a lowly position as a servant.

It didn't take too long before we arrived at a large house with iron gates at the entrance to its drive. We were met at the door by a middle aged woman who had obviously been on the lookout for Thomas' arrival.

Thomas and the lady greeted each other with little enthusiasm or love. As we were being shown into the house a man, who I also thought I had seen at the pub, ran through the open gate and immediately embraced the lady.

"Hello John. It is good to see you. Are you staying with us tonight?"
"Yes, if possible," came the reply.

Thomas smiled at the interruption as if resigned to the fact that this younger man was more important to the lady than he and his visitors.

"This is John Wright, a very good friend of mine and Martha's brother" he addressed us in a very matter of fact manner.

The sullen man brushed past the group and ran into the house, again hardly the actions of a servant.

Thomas continued with the introductions.

"This is my wife, Martha. Martha, these are friends of mine. They have done a lot of travelling and are staying with us for a few days. This is Grace, and this is John and this is . . . ." There was a pause as it was clear that, since he had no interest in the little girl, he had not remembered her name.

"I'm Eva."

"Yes, this is Eva and the young child is called er . . . ."

"Valentine!"

Eva was clearly annoyed!

"Yes. Valentine."

Martha looked suspiciously at us. We must have looked a strange bunch. However, eventually she smiled and invited us into a large entrance hall.

Up to this point Valentine had been incredibly quiet given the experiences he had been through, however he chose that moment to whimper as if to let us know that he was tired of all the 'goings on'. The whimper then changed into a full blooded cry and Martha took control.

"Come with me Eva," she said, taking Valentine from me. "I have some food and drink for you. You must be hungry after all the travelling that you have done."

If only she knew how far we had travelled, in the fourth dimension that is!

After Martha had left in what I presumed was the direction of the kitchen, Thomas led Grace, John and myself into an even larger lounge-type room.

"Would you like a drink?" he asked.
"No thank you," said John "I have had enough for today. Tell me sir, where have you and this pretty young lady travelled from?"

Before I had time to answer, Grace replied, "York".

York was not a good answer since we were attempting to return young Valentine to his mother at Great Staughton Manor on the border between Bedfordshire and Cambridgeshire and therefore would not be passing through London. However, it evoked an enthusiastic response from John Wright.

"That's where I went to school, St Peter's School on the banks of the River Ouse! My family lived on the East coast near Hull."

This situation seemed to be fraught with danger that maybe Grace did not fully understand but I couldn't stop her.

"I know that school! I live quite close to it and I have been in it giving Road Safety lessons to the pupils; I'm a police . . . ." her voice trailed off as she realised what she had said.

There was one of those deafening silences whilst all four of us considered what had been said from our own standpoint, although what John and Thomas made of Road Safety lessons was anybody's guess, let alone a woman in the police force. Did they have a police force in 1605? I wasn't sure!

John spoke first "You are a teacher? But what is the meaning of this subject called Road Safety?"

I managed to get in before Grace got herself into more deep water. "It is something that they are trying to introduce in York to make children aware of the dangers of horses and carriages on the streets. There have been several nasty accidents where children have been killed and injured because they are not aware of the dangers on those streets. York is a very busy place."

I was guessing, but it was the best I could come up with.

John agreed, a little reluctantly it seemed "Yes, York has become a very busy place."

"I would like a drink of water, sir, if that is possible?" Grace had recovered somewhat from her self-inflicted ordeal.
"Yes, of course, my dear. Johnson!" Thomas shouted in a very loud voice. The sullen Johnson arrived shortly after and was dispatched to get Grace a drink of water.

From then on Grace was a little more cautious about what she said, which in truth was very little and the rest of the time John and Thomas did most of the talking with the odd question thrown in. John spoke about his life in Yorkshire.

He was 36 years old and had been born at Plowland Hall in the village of Welwick in Holderness. He had a younger brother called Christopher and although his parents, Robert and Ursula, had called him John, most people referred to him as Jack.

He, like Thomas, was a staunch Catholic and didn't like the way the new King James was dealing with the many Catholics that lived in the new Great Britain as it was being called. It appeared to them that James was just carrying on the persecution of them just as Queen Elizabeth had done before him. In fact John's parents had suffered imprisonment for fourteen years in Hull Prison at the hands of Henry Hastings, the Puritan Earl of Huntingdon who was the Lord President of the North.

The lady we met at the door, Martha, was John's sister and she had married Thomas some thirteen years before. John and Thomas had become very good friends, united by marriage and by the Catholic faith.

John boasted of being the best swordsman in England and this brought a wry smile to Thomas' face. He was obviously very proud of his daring and courageous escapades in various rebellions in which he had been involved as a young man. Grace seemed captivated by John's stories although Thomas appeared less so. However, John seemed to be a pleasant man with a good sense of humour, although with a slow way of speaking and recounting his stories. This reminded me of a number of my friends. They told tales which went backwards in time rather than forward and were so long that you lost the will to live!

Prior to the one such rebellion in 1601 however, John, his brother Christopher, and a number of their friends were arrested during an illness of Queen Elizabeth. They were accused of plotting to poison her. However, according to John, no evidence of a plot or conspiracy was 'ever truly uncovered' that implicated either of the brothers or their friends. But John still spent an amount of time imprisoned in solitary confinement.

After his release, he had decided to move his family from the ancestral home of Plowland Hall to Twigmore Hall in Lincolnshire, which John proudly boasted had become a Catholic College for all 'who so wished'. Queen Elizabeth might not have looked on it in such a way, more likely, a place for Popish traitors to plot her downfall.

Thomas had kept fairly quiet throughout all this bravado and was intently watching Grace's expressions and probably admiring her pretty face.
He did mention that he had gone to Peterhouse College in Cambridge and had for a time, before James came to the throne after Elizabeth's death, been quite close to the then King James VI of Scotland. However, like John, he had become disenchanted by

the way King James I of England was treating those in the Catholic Church.

Thomas told us that his father was Edward Percy of Beverley. At least this time Grace kept quiet and refrained from informing us that she had shopped at Tesco's supermarket in Beverley or gone by train to Beverley races, or even worse arrested someone who had an ASBO for smoking grass outside the Queen Victoria pub!

I had tired of all this information and asked if I could be shown to where I could rest. Another loud shout for Johnson meant that I could follow the servant, leaving Thomas, John and Grace to, hopefully, talk further about things relating to the 17th Century and not the 21st! I hadn't been in the room more than a couple of minutes when there was a tentative knock at the door. It was Martha with Eva and a clean but tired-looking Valentine.

"The young master has settled, sir," she said tentatively, handing him over to me. I placed a very sleepy-looking Valentine onto the bed.

"Thank you. How has Eva been behaving?"
This brought a smile to Martha's face and a grimace from Eva.
"Fine sir. She's a real little lady."
A smile from me and another grimace from Eva, probably concerning both concepts of 'little' and 'lady'.
Martha departed.

Eva became animated. "There's something very funny going on in this house!"

"What do you mean?"

"Well," said Eva and 'well' always preceded a long, fast dialogue.

"Nice and steady."

She took a deep breath. "Well, a man called Robert came in at the side door to see that horrible servant Johnson, but he didn't call him John. He called him some foreign name like Geed. He must be an illegal immigrant and they must be hiding him here because they wouldn't let Martha and me listen to what they were saying. They just whispered to each other and it wasn't in English either. Some foreign language I didn't understand. When this Robert left with Johnson or whatever his name is, I asked Martha what they were whispering about and she got really embarrassed and said it wasn't anything, but it was. It seemed real serious, as if they were plotting to do something in secret. What do you think we should do, John?"

She took a breath.

"Nothing, it's none of our business. We have enough to worry about besides illegal immigrants being stowed away in this house."

"It might be one of those slave trade things we did in history once. You know, black market stuff."

"I think you are getting carried away a little."

"You are treating me like a little kid again just like Martha said," she sulked.

"No, I am not. We need to sort out our mess first and what we are going to do."

"We could go to the police!"

"I am not sure that they have been invented yet!"

"What, no police!"

"I don't think so. Have you seen Grace recently?" trying to change the subject.

"Yes, she is still talking to Thomas and John. Do you think they are in on this 'slave smuggling' racket?"

"No, they are very religious men. They wouldn't get involved in that sort of thing."

I could tell that Eva was not so convinced but the matter ended there as there was another knock at the door. It was Grace. She had managed to excuse herself from the conversations with Thomas and John and had been shown to her room across the hallway.

"Martha must have decided that Eva and I are sisters and we are sharing the same room," she said as she entered.

"Yes, and I have custody of Valentine. Sorry officer, not a good choice of words!"

Grace smiled.

Eva started to tell Grace about her suspicions and I decided it was time to go and have a word with Martha about food for Valentine and for the rest of us!

I found her in the kitchen with a young serving girl and a person I assumed was a cook. After apologizing for the interruption and explaining what I needed to know, Martha introduced the cook, Bertha, to me and said that anything I needed would be provided. Martha appeared nervous and anxious to get rid of me, so

I asked Bertha if we might have a little supper and would it be alright for it to be brought to our rooms as we were very tired. The men might think this a little rude but it was getting late and we really did need to talk in private about what our plans might be.

The plot thickens

After we had eaten the food provided for us and whilst Valentine slept as snug as a bug in the proverbial rug, the three of us started to discuss our options. The problem was that we all had different agendas and ideas of what to do next. In a nutshell, Eva wanted to get Valentine back to Staughton Manor and to his mother Hester then go home; Grace wanted to go home straight away; and I wanted anything that would get me out of the mess I was in and keep me out of a long jail sentence and for things to return to 'normal'.

"How is Eva able to get us back to 2008?" This question was directed at me but, as ever, Eva wasn't going to be treated as some child who would remain silent.
"That's easy! We find a ghost and enter their 'corridor of transit'. Don't you listen to anything we tell you?"

Grace did well not to reply in the sort of way a policewoman might do after a ticking off by a newly-qualified teenager! She seemed a little chastened but rallied.

"Where will we find a ghost?"

"Everywhere and anywhere" replied Eva

"Is . . . is there one in this room now?" Grace stammered a little.

"No, there isn't. I will tell you when there is and we are not going back to 2008 until we have done the good thing of returning Valentine to his mother."

"She hasn't seen him for over a year. How are you going to prove it's her child when you turn up unannounced?"

Eva thought for a moment. "She just will know. Every mother knows her child!"

"I'm with Eva on this. We have come too far to turn back. It's not too far to Bedford, about sixty miles."

"How do we travel to Bedford?"

"John steals horses!" Eva had a big smile on her face. The statement was true. I had stolen a horse and carriage on one occasion but the circumstances were that it had been necessary in order to stop us having to walk about 200 miles. As a bold statement of fact in front of a police officer, it did seem a little harsh. I started my defence but, as the old motto goes, when in a hole stop digging!

"I had to steal that lady's horse and carriage because you were getting tired of walking."

"You still shouldn't steal other people's possessions, John. It is not right and doesn't set a good example for Eva to follow."

"But she . . ." no, it was no good, I wasn't going to win. "Let's concentrate on our present situation," and I gave Eva a look which should have said 'I will get my own back later!'

"I suppose if we don't steal things we have to earn some money to pay for them. How can we earn enough money to get a lift to Bedford? It's easy to walk from Bedford to Great Staughton. John and I have done it before."

This was not quite true. We had bought a horse which Eva had called Cropredy since that was the village we had bought him in and had ridden him most of the way from Banbury to Great Staughton.

"Thomas is quite willing to let us stay here as long as we want," said Grace. Eva and I looked at each other as if to say 'we think we know why!' But at least if that was true we would have more time to find a more honest way of paying for our transport.

"I could always work behind a bar at one of those taverns," said Grace.
"I could go back and ask Henry if he could get us some money!"

All positive suggestions and they seemed to suggest a way forward. Whether it was the presence of a policewoman or not, we were going to do things the honest way and pay for our ticket to Great Staughton. The problem that the two ladies had overlooked was that we needed to get there after 1642 and we were still in 1605. So, although the sixty miles seemed no problem the thirty-seven years difference might prove to be a more difficult obstacle to overcome.

"John, what do you think of Eva's worries about what's going on in this house?" Grace changed the direction of the conversation.

"I agree that the longer we stay here the more of a problem it might become but for the moment you are better letting your detective instincts take a back seat."

A number of days passed and, as Grace had said, most of the household didn't seem to mind us staying. In fact, Martha became very friendly with Eva who spent a lot of time playing with her two children, Emma and Robert. This made Martha's life a lot easier. Despite the size of the house Thomas and Martha didn't seem to have all the trappings of the really rich. Although they had only a few servants, they did have a tutor who came in daily during the week to teach the children. He was a Catholic priest by the name of Father Hart, who had a kindly disposition and was not as austere as one might imagine of a teacher of that time. Emma and Robert seemed to look forward to their lessons, and in a way so did Eva who never missed an opportunity to 'help' Father Hart in his task!

Grace was spending more and more time with Thomas, worryingly so. However he did seem to spend quite a lot of time away from the house and occasionally he took Grace with him. On a number of occasions I thought of having a word with her about the situation, but then again she was old enough to look after herself.

There were a number of men who frequently visited the house to talk to either Thomas or John, or both. John was staying in the house for the time-being, presumably visiting his sister, of whom he was clearly very fond.

The Robert that Eva had seen was a frequent visitor, along with a man called Thomas Wintour and occasionally Christopher, who was the younger brother of John and Martha. There was, however, no sign of illegal immigrants or foreigners of any description, apart from the sullen Johnson.

One afternoon I returned from a walk in the pleasant spring sunshine, to be met by a very excited Eva.

"I know what's going on! Robert and Emma told me something about what I did at school!" This didn't make any sense!

"Told you what?"

"It's not smuggling, it's a plot. All those men that keep coming and talking to Thomas and that servant Johnson. That's not his name you know!"

"Calm down and start at the beginning!"

"We were having a lesson with Father Hart about different religions and he said that the country that the servant Johnson came from was mainly Catholic whereas here it's mainly Protestant, or something like that, and then Robert said that the servant's name wasn't Johnson but Fawkes!! John, we are living in the same house as Guy Fawkes!!"

It took some time to sink in but the dates were about right, November 5th, 1605 'Gunpowder Plot'!

"Steady on Eva. You said the man that came the other day called him Geed."

"It was Guido, not Geed, and that is Spanish for Guy! That man in there is the same one we burnt in our back garden last year and come to think of it, every year I can remember."

"OK, so what?"

"So what! If we want, we can stop the 'Gunpowder Plot'."

"Whoa! We can't meddle in the history of England. That's not the reason we came here and why would you want to spoil 'Bonfire Night' for all those children?"

"Yes, that's a point, but these men are plotting to kill the King."

"Yes, but we know that they don't succeed, don't we?"

"OK, but what are we going to do?"

"I suggest nothing and leave here as soon as possible. We have about seven months to make our departure. What am I saying! We want to get back to normal as soon as possible and with Grace's help I can be a free man again."

"Typical of you, John! Me, me and me."

"OK, I am being selfish, but may I remind you, you got us into this mess in the first place."

"If it wasn't for my quick thinking you'd be doing twenty years in Hull Prison like Martha's poor mum, Ursula. The only difference being she was being persecuted for being a Catholic, whereas you would be in for kidnapping two children!"

"Why you ungrateful . . . . You wanted to help Valentine's dad out in the first place, not me."

This was getting childish, but to her credit it was Eva who brought an end to this tit-for-tat mud slinging.

"OK, you are right there, but what would we do if we found out that a Spaniard was going to blow up our Queen Elizabeth?"

"OK, what do YOU suggest we do?"

"Well, what do we know about the 'Gunpowder Plot'? We know that Guy Fawkes plants lots of gunpowder under the Houses of Parliament with the idea of blowing up King James on November 5th in 1605. He obviously has some helpers; Thomas, John, his brother Christopher and that Robert and his mate

Thomas Wintour and come to think of it all those other men sat around the table in the Duck and Drake."

"You might find that there are 13 conspirators."
"Con what?"

"I think that there were thirteen people involved in the plot. They were all caught and hung for trying to blow up King James."
"That's sad 'cos I like John and Christopher. Are we going to tell Grace what we have found out? She's in love with Thomas I think."
What an observation from a thirteen-year-old!

"I think love is a bit strong. I know she likes him a lot, but love?"
"You men know nothing about love, do you?"
"OK, less of the analysis. I think that we should keep this to ourselves. She might not believe that the man she is supposedly in love with is trying to blow up the King and furthermore meets his death in a little over seven months' time."

Grace and Thomas

Grace did in fact find a job of some sort, although I suspect Thomas had arranged it with one of his network of friends. She became very secretive about what she was doing and didn't like either Eva or I prying into her life. It was clear that she had become somewhat obsessed with Thomas and he, in turn, was captivated by the much younger woman with the beautiful face.

I am not particularly good at describing people. I would, it is fair to say, be useless at helping the police with an Identikit picture of a thief I had seen, but as I said before Thomas was a tall, physically impressive man, with an attractive manner. He was in his forties and was prematurely going grey. His main problem was that he was prone to sweat a lot and often had to change his shirt, sometimes three times a day. Consequently, he had some kind of skin problem which was so acute that he could only wear shirts of the finest material and spent quite a lot of time shopping for them. Often he would take Grace with him on these and other expeditions.

Eva spent most of the days playing with Martha's and Thomas' two children, Robert and Emma. Robert was a couple of years younger than Eva and Emma often reminded us that she was nine years old and nearly ten.

The three played particularly well with Valentine and the bond between him and Eva grew ever stronger, so much so that tears would flow if Eva left him for any period of time. Circumstances had meant that they had spent a lot of time together, even when Valentine had been put into care when the authorities had decided to try and locate his parents. Fat chance they had of that ever happening!

Mostly they played in a special room set aside as a teaching and play room for the two Percy children. When the weather was good they would play out in the garden, if their father permitted it. He seemed a strict unloving father whom the children (Eva excepted) feared and often they cowered in his presence. It is really sad that children grew up that way.

Eva was like a little ray of sunshine in their lives. She was a very different child from those with whom they normally played. I hoped that Eva had not introduced them to her sinister world of ghosts and the living dead. I left Eva to do what she did best and I tried to formulate some kind of plan for our journey to Great Staughton to return Valentine to his mother.

I was in the middle of such a plan when my room door opened and an agitated Eva entered.

"She's gone!"
"Who's gone and where?"

"Grace has gone. All her belongings have disappeared from the room and I cannot find her."
"Maybe she's at work?"
"Why would she take all the clothes that Thomas has bought her to work? I think she has run off with him somewhere. What are we going to do?"

"I'll go and ask Martha where Thomas has gone. I'm sure that there must be a simple explanation."
"Yes, there is. The stupid woman has gone and fallen in love with someone born four hundred years before she was and has run off with him, goodness knows where!"

"How are we going to find her?" Eva continued "We cannot just leave her in the 17th century can we? We have to find her!"

I went to find Martha to see if indeed there was a simple explanation. I eventually found her in the library. It was evident that she had been crying, although she did her best to cover it up.

"Do you know where Grace is, Martha?"

She didn't answer for a time. She probably didn't know what to say. Eventually she said, "She and Thomas have gone to stay at Hampton Court as guests. Thomas says that there are some important people meeting there."

"Why has he taken Grace?"
She gave me a look that required no words and then broke down in tears again.
"Thomas doesn't want me any more. Grace is younger and prettier than I am," she sobbed. "He says that he has fallen in love with her!"
"He cannot fall in love with her, she's from a different time," I blurted.

"What do you mean?"
"Sorry I cannot explain that now but can you tell me how to get to Hampton Court?"
"They won't allow you in. It's for special guests only, royalty and people of high rank. There will be guards on the gates."
"Please just give me directions there and I will try to get them to come back."

"He says that he doesn't want me anymore and is leaving for good with that girl. What can I do? I have Emma and Robert to look after and no money. Thomas pays for everything and he says that he will not give us another penny. What am I going to do?"

There are times when words are no good, so I put my arms around her and hoped that my wife would understand, given the circumstances.

When I returned to my room, Eva was playing with Valentine. He was such a happy child. It was hard to believe that, given the difficult and strange times he had lived through in his short life, he could be so contented. He loved Eva and it was not going to be easy for Eva to part with him, even if we did manage to return him to his mother.

"Did you find anything out?" she asked.
"A little. Thomas and Grace have gone to stay at Hampton Court."
"I've heard of that place. Wasn't it something to do with Henry VIII?"
"Yes, I think so."
"And all those wives!"
"Six of them, to be exact."
"Why would a man want six wives?"

It was a question I could have answered but it would have taken a lot of explanation. I left the question unanswered.

"We need to go to Hampton Court and try and talk some sense into Grace."
"Do we tell her that her beloved Thomas is going to try and blow up the King and gets killed for his troubles?"
"It's a pity we don't have the history book that I brought on the last trip. It would tell us when and where he dies. That might shock Grace into being sensible again!"

The 17th century history book that I had brought with us on our last visit had indeed been helpful, although at

41

times, knowing what was going to happen had made us sad and apprehensive.

Suddenly, Eva disappeared and in minutes she was back triumphantly holding the book in her hands. "Do you mean this book might be helpful?"

"Well done Eva! That book might turn out to be just what we need to bring Grace to her senses. Have you been carrying it around in that rucksack all this time?"
"Yes, I am not such a weakling as you make out."

"OK, we can look at the book later. Right now we need to make plans for our visit to Hampton Court. Martha has given me some directions but it is about fourteen miles away."
"How long a walk is that?"
"About six hours at our pace. If we were good marathon runners we could do it in just over an hour!"
"Or if we steal a horse and carriage even less!"

"Didn't you give me a lecture on being honest this time around?"
"Yes, but that was before we had to walk fourteen miles!"

Suddenly, we could hear raised voices coming from the floor below. Someone was really upset and it wasn't a woman's voice that was making all the noise.
"I'll take a look downstairs," I said.
"I'll come too," replied Eva, not wishing to be left out.

The voices were coming from the entrance hall. The angry voice was that of John Wright and the quieter one that of his sister Martha. Clearly she had told him of the elopement of Thomas and Grace and quite rightly John was a bit angry.

He stopped mid-sentence as he saw us descending the stairs.
"We want to help find Grace," Eva's voice sounded very determined.

John seemed unsure as to whether he could take advice from a thirteen-year-old girl and his reply had more than a little sarcasm in it.
"How do you propose to help? You don't come from around these parts, in fact we have no idea who you are or where you have come from."

Eva was a girl older than her years. "Yes, but Grace is my sister and I love her and I want her back so we can go on our way without trouble."
This took the wind right out of John's sails. "I'm sorry, I wasn't thinking. Of course you can help, but you have to understand how serious this is."

"Oh, I think we do know," Eva replied and for a moment I thought that she was going to add "because it messes up all your 'Gunpowder Plot' plans," but she didn't.

"What do you think we should do?" John seemed to be addressing this question to Martha but as ever it was Eva who replied.

"We need to go to Hampton Court and kidnap Grace and take her away so that she can come to her senses!"

"Sounds like a good plan," I added so as to give the plan a bit more credibility.

"They wouldn't let us in," said John, trying to put a dampener on things.

"You take us there and leave the rest to my father and me. We will take responsibility for the kidnap and if we get caught we will not mention you helped us. All we want you to do, Mr Wright, is to take us to Hampton Court."

It was plain to see John was taken aback by the forthrightness of what he had just heard and I still found any reference to me being Eva's father a touch unbelievable given the age difference. On our previous visit to the 17th century we had decided I was to be her grandfather so promotion to father was quite something!

"Indeed, I can take you to Hampton Court but I do not see how you will be able to get past the guards that are in place there."

"Please Mr Wright; give us the chance to rescue my sister from Mr Percy."

What a way she has with words! A hint of the fact that Mr Percy is an evil man from whom her sister must be rescued.

"Yes, I will but I cannot do it straight away, I have business to attend to today. Maybe we can travel there tomorrow." John's anger at his brother-in-law's infidelity seemed to have subsided a little with the prospect of the kidnapping of Grace.

Eva and I made our way back to the room given to her and Grace. At least we had a bit of time to talk over a plan, although I didn't think I would have much of a say in it. We had rescued two small children in similar, although less guarded circumstances, before. The executed plan had been all Eva's!

"We could do with a map of Hampton Court," Eva said, once we thought no one could hear us.

"I have been to Hampton Court a few times, although my last visit was some time ago. My best friend from school, Bob, lives in Long Ditton and every time we visited him and his lovely wife Nancy, we made a trip to Hampton Court. Bob really liked the subject of History at school and what is more their daughter Tracey worked there for a number of years."

"Is any of this helpful to us at the moment?"
"Well, only if I can remember the layout of the palace. I hope that it was the same in the 17th century as it was when we visited it."
"Unlikely, but give it go. What do you remember about it?"

"Big courtyard, quite a few rooms for storing food and preparing it for Henry VIII, lots of rooms for the guests he had staying there, and oh yes, lots of rumours about ghosts walking the corridors!"

"Sounds perfect!"
"There were some rooms to do with Edward, his son, I think. It's best we just get there and then see what we can do."
"Who were the ghosts suppose to be?"
"Er . . . let me think; two of Henry's wives, Catherine Howard and Jane Seymour, were supposed to have been seen there."

"Are they dead now in 1605?"
"Oh yes. Jane Seymour died after giving birth to Edward, so that would be about 1535ish and Catherine was beheaded about five years later. She was wife number five whilst Jane I think was number three."

"What was Catherine beheaded for?"
"She probably upset Henry."
"My Dad didn't have Mum beheaded when she upset him about not wanting him to go to rugby!"

"Slightly different in the 17th century. Henry did anything he wanted, including having people beheaded if they upset him. He was very powerful. He even went against the Pope so that he could divorce his first wife."
"Why was that?"
"Well, they were all Catholics and Catholics are not allowed to be divorced from their wives."

"Ok. Any more likely ghosts?"

"Oh yes, apparently there was a phantom dog and the ghost of a cat."

"They won't be much use."

"None of them might be as they may be just tales."

"We'll just have to go and find out for ourselves then, I guess."

Hampton Court

John Wright, despite the bravado he had shown in front of Grace and Thomas, appeared to be a very pleasant young man with very definite views on how the Catholic Church should be treated by the King. He talked for most of the three and a half hour journey for which he had kindly hired and paid. I had forgotten how painful and uncomfortable riding by horse and carriage on 17th century roads had been. Eva seemed quite at home as we clip-clopped our way south towards Hampton Court.

I detected a note of nervousness in his voice as he talked about what Thomas had done in running off with Grace and how his sister had reacted. It was clear that he feared Thomas Percy and feared what Thomas might say if he knew that he had any part in what he was now doing in taking us to Hampton Court. He repeatedly said that what he was doing was for his sister and no other reason.

Knowing what Eva and I knew about the 'Gunpowder Plot' and what was going to happen to poor John, it was difficult not to feel sorry for him. He was going to die a violent death at a young age, although we had no idea where or when, except it would be after the 5th November this year.

He shouted to the driver to stop the carriage some distance from Hampton Court. I assumed that he didn't want to be seen too close to the Palace as it might raise awkward questions.

"The Palace is half a mile down that road yonder." He pointed towards another rough cobbled road and then he said belatedly, "and don't mention that I had anything to do with bringing you down here. Understood?"

We both nodded. It wasn't our intention to get John into any trouble after the kindness he had shown in helping us and hopefully, indirectly, his sister Martha.

"We'll do what we have to do and you will never see us again." Eva was confident in our success much more than I was. John smiled, probably thinking the same of how one so young could be so confident in the outcome of such a difficult task.

"Good luck!" he shouted as the carriage turned around and headed back to Westminster.

Eva and I stood beside the road for a moment. "What do you think is our best plan John?"

I had to smile because I hadn't a clue. We had been in this kind of situation before and usually it was Eva who found a magical solution.

"Are there any people around that you can see that I cannot?" It must have ranked as one of the dumbest questions I had ever asked.
"How do I know? I can see everybody, dead or alive."
"OK, stupid question. Can you see a group of women over there?"
"Yes!"
"and those children?"
"Yes!"

"What about the old man near the tree?"
"Why are we doing this? It should be me asking you not the other way around. Remember I can see everybody."

"OK, that's all the people I can see at present. Oh, wait a minute, there are two children playing a game just behind that tree."
"Let's go have a word with them; they're much more likely to help us."
"Why?" I asked.
"Because I am a child of about the same age as that girl over there and she is much more likely to tell me the things that I need to know than the adults. You can be a bit thick at times, John," and she was gone, running in the direction of the two children.

I slowly made my way after her and by the time I had caught up with her she was deep in conversation with the girl who was clearly the older of the two children.

"This is Charlotte," Eva said, as I approached "and that is her little brother Jacob."

Although it was difficult to tell with them both dressed in what could only be described as rags with no shoes, Jacob was about ten years old and Charlotte was probably Eva's age.

"This is my grandfather, John," Eva continued, "and we want to go into Hampton Court to meet someone but we are not sure if they'll let us in." Demoted to grandfather once again!

"No, they don't allow strangers in, only nobles and people who work there like my mother."
"What does your mother do?"
"She works in the kitchens."
"And your father?"
"He died of the plague last year."
"Oh, I'm so sorry."

Charlotte seemed a bit taken aback at Eva's sympathy. Probably because so many people had died during the last few years, death was just a common part of life.

"Is there any way that we can get into the Palace without being seen by the guards?"

"I don't think so," replied Charlotte, "they are having some kind of gathering with lots of important people from all over London."

Jacob, who on my arrival had cowered behind his sister, suddenly appeared from behind her skirts and spoke. "I know how we can get into the Court."
"No, you don't. Stop telling lies, Jacob!"
"But I do, Charlotte. There's a drain that runs from the Base Court into the river."
"But that's full of rats, and they would bite you and you would die of the plague!"
"The rats don't come out so much in the day, only at night. I have been down the drain lots of times and not been bitten."
"No, you haven't."
"Yes, I have."
"OK," Eva said, interrupting the brother-sister argument, "how wide is this drain, Jacob?"
"You could go down it but not the mister."

"Look, we have got some food we could give you if you could show us how to get in." Eva produced some of the food that Martha had prepared for us. They both looked at us and then stared at the food Eva was offering. They looked as if they hadn't eaten much as they were both incredibly thin.

"It wouldn't be safe, Eva. Remember you haven't had some of the jabs that would make you immune from a rat bite and the plague."

Charlotte and Jacob looked puzzled at the language that I had just used but it wasn't worth explaining to them.

"Has anybody died recently in the Palace?"

Most people would have considered Eva's question as bizarre but the children didn't seem phased by it. The number of deaths from the recent plague made life quite cheap and death was part of life for these poor children.

They looked at each other as if they were not sure what to tell us.
"Our sister has just died, that's why our ma wants us to play out here. She's planning Amy's funeral."
"Where was your sister born?" Another strange question but Charlotte obliged.
"In the servant quarters in the Palace like me and Jacob. Why?"
"Oh, no reason," Eva lied.

"It's getting very foggy. Does the fog come most days?"
"Yes. Some people say it's to do with burning coal but they get it much worse near the docks in London. It comes down most days."
"How will you get back into the Palace?" I asked.
"The guards know us so they let us in. Come on Jacob, it's time we returned to the kitchens. Goodbye," and with that they ran away towards the Palace.

"It looks like the drain then?" Eva said.
"I don't think that's a good idea."

"Have you got a better one?"
"We must be able to think of something."

"I know. Do you remember that time in Nottingham when I scared that horrible soldier with Purkiss?"
Purkiss had been a magnificent stag that had saved our lives on a number of occasions on our earlier trip into this century but sadly he had died on one such occasion.

"Yes, I remember it well. We got locked up in a dungeon for quite a time."
"Oh yes, we did, didn't we. Well, anything else?"

"Maybe, Charlotte said her sister had just died and that they were preparing a funeral. That would need an undertaker. Maybe a bit of acting might get us past the guard."
"You are old enough to be an undertaker and certainly look like one, but who am I going to be?"

"Any more complements like that and the sewerage drain looks like a good option for you."
"Is that what it would be, a sewerage drain?"
"What did you think it would be; a river of rose petals? You can be thick sometimes." I smiled and Eva grinned.

"I suppose I could be your granddaughter and you are looking after me."
"Never a truer word has passed your lips."
"What was that supposed to mean?"

"OK, let's go try our luck with the guards. I think there is some kind of clock tower near the front of the Palace and if I remember correctly, the kitchens are to the left when we get through the main courtyard."

To say the guards looked a bit mean would be an understatement. They eyed us with suspicion as we approached them.
"What is your business here?"

"There has been a death in the Palace, caused by the plague, and I have come to take the body away as soon as possible so others won't catch it." This seemed the most direct way of scaring them into letting us pass. I also assumed that they would not be medically trained as I was pretty sure, but not absolutely certain, that you couldn't catch the plague from a dead body.

"Who's died? Nobody has told us of any death."
"I suppose that they wouldn't want to scare anybody at this time, particularly with King James having invited so many guests."

"I don't believe him," interjected the other guard. "They would have told us if someone was collecting a body."

"But if the King dies of the plague just because you wouldn't let us in to remove the disease from the Palace, then we will tell them who was responsible for the King's death!" Just the right amount of malice to make them think.

It did the trick. They looked at each other and came to a compromise. "William here will go with you," said the first guard, although William looked as if the compromise was not to his liking.

"Where is the body?"
"All we know is that it is a young girl whose mother works in the kitchens."
"Which one? We have lots of kitchens in the Palace."
I took a chance. "The one where the King's food is prepared."
"Follow me."

We went into a large courtyard and turned left and followed him under an arch. As we did, I noticed a large clock. I couldn't remember exactly what it was but I had a recollection that there was something strange about that clock.

"What are we going to do to get rid of him?" whispered Eva.
"Get rid of who?" I said, still thinking about the clock.
"Father Christmas, who do you think?" she hissed.
"Oh, the guard."
"Yes, the guard." The same guard that now stood glaring at us.
"What are you whispering about!"

"We have never been in this Palace before and we were talking about the clock we have just passed." It was the best answer I could give.

"Oh that," he said proudly. "That is the Astronomical Clock made for King Henry. It shows the hour of the day, the month, the day of the month and," with mounting pride, "the phases of the moon. It is the finest clock in the world!"

"It also seems to show that the sun revolves around the earth!" Eva smiled.

"That's right, because it does," the guard confirmed. Eva gave me one of her special looks but said nothing further. Those scientists like Galileo would also have been smiling had they been born yet. Eva knew it was not the time to enlighten the guard. We needed to get rid of him.

Suddenly, Eva stumbled and fell on the cobbled stones. She was up to something. The fall was a little too staged. She held up her hand to stop me from giving her any assistance and beckoned to the guard.

"I think I've hurt my ankle," she said to him as he approached. She offered her hand to him and, in the spirit of kindness that up to now hadn't been shown, he helped her to her feet.

"Who is that lady stood by the doorway in the white dress? She seems upset," Eva asked.

Whoever Eva was pointing at, I had no idea. I couldn't see anybody by the door. One thing was certain, if the lady was upset, it was nothing to how the guard was reacting. He gave out an almighty scream and ran back through the archway into the courtyard. Now was our chance to disappear. I still had no idea what Eva had shown the guard, but I guessed it was either gruesome or shocking in some way. It wasn't the time to ask Eva what had happened, we must somehow disappear.

We ran towards the door where, I assumed, the lady was standing. I might have passed right through her for all I knew. Fortunately, I wasn't in contact with Eva at the time, so ignorance was indeed bliss.

The door led into a short corridor and the stench of raw meat hit me straight away. The rooms to our right clearly held meat for the King's table.

"Where now?" Eva asked.
"I think we need to go left at the end of this corridor and that takes us round to the main kitchens." I was wrong. It had changed somewhat in the period between 1605 and when I visited it last.

"We need to slow down and act calmly."
A woman came out of a door to our left. This time it was a real woman. She was heading towards us. She smiled as she passed.

"Excuse me. Could you tell us where we can find the mother of Charlotte and Jacob? We have a message for her," Eva, as ever, was quick thinking.

"Well, I think I saw her about an hour ago in the main kitchen."

"Where exactly is that? I'm afraid this is our first visit to the Palace."

The woman looked quizzically at Eva and then at me.
"What is your business with Rebecca?"
"It's about the death of her daughter," I said, as solemnly as I could.
"Oh yes, poor Amy." There was a moment's silence as the lady thought about poor Amy. "You need to go through that door there, turn left and follow the passage to the right. At the end of that passage is the door to the main kitchen, Rebecca should be there."

We thanked her and quickly disappeared. Surely by the time the guard had calmed down and explained what he had seen, there would be a search for the young girl and her grandfather.

In truth we had no idea what our plan was but being inside the palace meant that we had a chance of seeing Grace and being able to talk her into leaving with us.

Delivering the manchet

I pushed the kitchen door open and was met with a blast of smelly hot air. A large log fire must have been close by, as you could hear the spitting and crackling coming from within. At first, it seemed as if there was no-one around. To our left there was what looked like an oven and on a table next to it rows of large pies, presumably with meat in them.

"They don't eat the crust of those pies, you know John."
Not exactly what I had expected Eva to say.
"Now is not the time to discuss 17th century pies, Eva!"
"The crust is only used as a container. You take it off and just eat the meat in it. The pastry is just flour and water and not like the pastry we have at home."

The history lesson came to a sudden end as a large man came down the few steps that entered the room from the other side.

"Ah! There you are at last. Take the manchet from the table up there to the Great Hall. They are waiting for it and you are late!"
"Yes sir. Straight away," I replied.

"What's that little girl doing here? She shouldn't be here."
"I heard that Charlotte and Jacob, Rebecca's children, had lost their sister Amy and thought Eva might be able to cheer them up." I was getting good at telling quick lies and to be truthful I didn't like the skill I had picked up.

"They are in the servant's kitchen. I will take the little girl to them. Rebecca could certainly do with someone to cheer her up. You get on your way with that manchet."

We had met 'manchet' on our previous visit and eaten quite a bit of it too. It was a wheat yeast sweetbread, eaten by those who were well off. I placed all the 'loaves' that the man handed to me into the basket and turned to go back the way we had come.
"Where are you going? It's that door to the Great Hall, stupid."
"Mind the cat, John!" shouted Eva.

The man and I looked at each other in amazement. There was no cat to be seen!
"Is she alright?" the man said in a tone of 'is she mad?'
"Yes. She has these turns of seeing things that are not there since she had a touch of the plague."

As soon as I said it I realized that it probably wasn't the right thing to have said.

"I'm ok now, grandad. Can I go and play with Charlotte and Jacob?"

The man seemed less willing to take her but crossed the room and opened the door to let her pass.

"On your way with that manchet!" he repeated. "That door up there!" He pointed to a door at the far end of the kitchen. I walked passed the roaring fire on which there was a large spit holding what look like a wild boar. In truth I would have been a bit wild if I was on a spit in that position!

I hadn't a clue where I was going. I thought I knew the way to the Great Hall but that was back from where we had come and through the Clock courtyard, but this way was a mystery to me. I wasn't dressed as if I was a guest of the King, more a cross between a servant and a 'down and out'. It might be an idea to knock out one of the guards and steal his clothes. I had seen it done many times on film and it always looked so easy, but when you come down to it, how do you go about it? Although I had been knocked out several times myself, on a rugby field, I definitely had not knowingly knocked someone else out. Do you use a piece of wood? I didn't think that I was strong enough to punch somebody's 'lights out'. No it wouldn't feel right. These clothes would have to do.

If I could get to the Great Hall quickly, drop the manchet with somebody, I would have a little time on the way back to look around and maybe find out where Grace and Thomas were. I wandered around for a bit, from one corridor to another, until I saw a group of women ahead and in the words of Pearl, my mother, 'you are never lost with a tongue in your head'.

"Excuse me ladies, I have just begun working here and have to deliver this manchet to the Great Hall. I seem to have got lost. Could you tell me the way?"

They all gave me a look which seemed to mean 'is this guy for real?', but the one that seemed to be the oldest, and better dressed of the three, smiled and said "Follow me, I am going that way. Goodbye you two, I will see you tonight in the Great Hall."

I followed her through two doors and out into what I recognized as the Clock courtyard and through an archway into another courtyard which contained a fountain which again was familiar. A vague recollection came into my head as to why King Henry VIII liked this Palace and allegedly stole it from Cardinal Wolsey. The sanitation was very good with lots of fresh running water available and therefore less of a health risk.

The lady stopped and turned to me. "You don't sound as if you come from the City of London. Where are you from?"

"Kingston upon Hull," I said confidently and then realized my mistake. Hull had not become a King's Town until King Charles bestowed the title on the city some years later. "It's in the north of England."

She seemed an educated woman and probably didn't 'buy' the Kingston upon Hull answer that I had given her. "I have never heard of that town."
"It's near the city of York, on the east coast of England," I hoped my clarification would stop anymore questions, but it didn't.

"What is your name?"
"John, and yours?"
"I am Helen Little. I look after the King's three children, Henry, Charles and Elizabeth."

"I am sorry, my lady, for my impertinence in speaking to you." This was me trying to be deferential!
"No matter, I was on my way to the Great Hall from the kitchen. But I am intrigued by your demeanour. You sound a learned man?"

"Well, my lady, I was a teacher of mathematics but have come to London to seek my fortune." What a pathetic answer. This wasn't some kind of pantomime. This could get serious.

"Why teaching is such a noble profession and particularly mathematics. I think that you have made a grave mistake coming to London when we have had such a great plague in our midst this last year. You would have been much safer in the north."

"You are correct my lady, but sometimes it is worth taking risks."

She gave me a look of pity. "The Great Hall is up those stairs there, through the large doors and to the right. You will need to speak to Robert; he is in charge of the arrangements for tonight. I bid you good afternoon," and she walked off to the right towards what looked like living apartments.

I gave a big sigh of relief. Helen was a shrewd lady and probably a bit suspicious, as many who surrounded the king and his children might be when encountering strangers.

I followed her instructions; 'up the stairs, through the large doors and to the right and Robert should be there'. The first three were carried out successfully but on turning right I walked straight into Grace. She was dressed immaculately and looked stunning in an 'off the shoulder' royal blue gown.

There was a moment when neither of us knew what to say.

"You have to come with me and leave Thomas. It's dangerous for you to stay with him." It was the best I could do.

"What do you mean 'dangerous'? Don't be silly! I have met King James today and lots of earls. We are perfectly safe here. It's truly beautiful here. I never believed I could be in Hampton Court dressed like this and in the presence of the King of England."

She was certainly awe-struck with the position she was in.

"It's not King James that is the problem, it's Thomas!"

"Don't be silly!" That was the third time, I think, that I'd been called silly or stupid that day and I was getting a bit 'brassed off' with it.

"You're coming with me!"

"No, I'm not."

I grabbed her arm and she screamed. Before I knew it I was grabbed from behind and felt a heavy blow to the back of my head and the world went black.

In search of a plan

I had been in many dungeons before, even in Alcatraz, but nearly all of the visits were done voluntarily. This one wasn't. I awoke in a very dark and dismal place with a pounding headache. I felt the back of my head where the pain was worst and it felt sticky. I had no real recollection of what had happened to me after I had met up with Grace.

The hours passed and I had no idea of what time of day it was or what day it was! Somebody had done to me what I was not capable of doing, rendering someone unconscious. I wondered what Eva was up to; whether she was ok by herself. What was I thinking; of course she would be alright, but maybe wondering what had happened to grandad!

I must have dropped off to sleep because I was awakened by some clanking of keys and opening of doors. I was dragged to my feet by two burly guards and marched through the door into the light. It must have been the next morning, or maybe the one after that.

I was confronted by the one person I didn't really want to see; Thomas Percy. Sweat poured from his brow, his skin disorder was giving him problems, or was it guilt? "What are you doing here, John?"
I wasn't in the mood for pleasantries. "Somebody hit me over the head and dragged me here."
"No, I mean, why are you here in Hampton Court Palace?"

"I could ask you the same question. What are you and Grace doing here when your wife Martha is at home?"

He was ruffled but kept his false pleasant demeanour. "We are here at the request of King James. It is a religious matter we are discussing; the possible formation of a new bible to be exact."

"And you need Grace to help you. Do you even know what religion she is?"
"I am not sure. Do you know what religion she follows?"
"No, I do not. She is old enough to make her own mind up."

"I ask again. Why have you come here, John?"
"To talk to Grace and I was doing just that when we were forcibly separated. Did you hit me, Thomas?"
"No, I was in conference at the time, but Grace tells me that you tried to force her to go away with you and the little girl."

"Where is Eva? Do you know?"

"Yes. She is safe and amusing some children, and adults, in the servants' quarters. She is quite a young lady by all accounts with a vivid imagination."

"Can I see her?"

"Will you then leave?"

"Yes, I suppose we will have to if you and King James say so. But what do you want me to tell Martha and her brother John?"

"Nothing for the moment. Grace and I are not sure of what we want to do. We are in love."

Yes, I bet they were; a rich and famous forty-something grey haired man with a serious skin complaint and a beautiful blonde twenty-five-year old who hadn't been born yet!

One possibility was that I should tell him the truth about our journey from the future; a second more devious thought was to tell him I knew about his 'Gunpowder Plot' to kill the king. Neither seemed a good plan.

"I would like to see Eva if I may," I said politely.

"Yes of course. Come this way."

I shrugged myself free of my two henchmen and without looking at them walked after Thomas. We walked across the courtyard with the fountain in it and up into a long hallway. Sitting at the far end were three children and two ladies. I recognized one of them as being Helen Little, the lady I had spoken to whilst trying to deliver the manchet. The three children were Eva,

Charlotte and Jacob. Eva ran towards me, arms open wide. I had never seen her so pleased to see me.

"What did they do to you?"
"Oh nothing," I said," I will tell you later," and should have added, 'when we plot our revenge'.
"I hope you are alright sir," the voice of a seemingly sympathetic Helen.
"Yes, thank you my lady, but it is a shame that, in a Palace of this nature, people are so violent towards strangers." I felt Thomas twitch nervously.

"This lady here is Rebecca, the mother of Charlotte and Jacob, but she has no recollection of asking anyone to come into the Palace to help bury her sadly deceased daughter Amy."

"Yes, I am sorry about that misunderstanding my lady, but Eva and I wanted to speak to Grace, the companion of Thomas here." I pointed in Thomas' direction. He twitched again.

"What do you want to speak to her about?"
"It is rather a private matter my lady but if you insist I can explain." Thomas twitched for a third time and no doubt his sweat increased.

"No matter," said Helen, "but I will get a doctor to look at that wound. I would like to make sure that you leave us with no permanent discomfort."
"You are very kind."

"You may leave us Thomas." He hesitated but felt uncomfortable enough to want to leave.

"May I have a brief word with my granddaughter?"
"By all means."

I slowly escorted Eva out of earshot of Helen and to my surprise Charlotte and Jacob followed. Charlotte then spoke the words I dreaded most. "We have seen ghosts. Eva can make us see them."

"I am sorry, Charlotte, but I would like to speak to Eva alone," and I motioned to Rebecca for help.
"Come with me you two and let Eva talk to her grandfather alone."
They followed Rebecca back to the end of the hallway.

"Dare I ask what you have been doing?"
"I could ask you the same."
"Come on, don't try and be smart with me," I said, "I know you too well."

"This place is seriously haunted, John. There are ghosts everywhere and two really nice ladies who have been very helpful. They say that they were Queens of England and then there was the cat you nearly trod on when you were carrying that bread!"

"You have seen the ghosts of animals in this place?"
"Well, just the cat and a dog. Anyway, what happened to you? You disappeared!"

I briefly explained what had happened and Eva sounded suitably annoyed with Grace's behaviour.
"What are we going to do?" she said.

"I was hoping that you might come up with something. We can't let Grace stay here, knowing what's going to happen to Thomas. She might get killed and then where would I be?"
"What do you mean, 'where will you be'?"

"What I mean is, if we do manage to get back to 2008, people will believe Grace when she tells them what has happened and I won't to go to prison."

"That is a slightly selfish way of saying you don't want her to die. Anyway they will believe me, won't they?"
"They didn't the last time, that's why we are in this predicament."
"Yes, but they do have the evidence of a whole court load of people seeing us disappear before their very eyes!"

"Yes, that is true. Anyway have you seen anything that might help us?"

"Jane might be able to help. She is a very sweet lady and sadly she died only two weeks after her son Edward was born here in the Palace.

This story had a familiar ring to it. "You mean you've met Jane Seymour, one of Henry VIII's wives?"

"Two actually! Catherine Howard's around as well, but mostly in a different place. She's Henry's fifth wife."

"Yes and Jane Seymour was his third."

"Divorced, beheaded, died, divorced, beheaded, survived. We did that in History in year eight. It's what happened to all Henry's six wives you know. The first was divorced, second . . ."

"Yes, I know all that. I was in year eight once you know." Not strictly true, they were numbered differently in my day, but Eva wouldn't have known that.

"You in year eight? That wasn't in this millennium!"

"Well clever clogs, it was. Since we are in the 17th century, you are the one who has never been in year eight in this millennium!"

Eva furrowed her brow and then smiled, "You're right!"

"How could Jane Seymour help us?"

"Well, she's always walking up and down the stairs that lead to the Clock Court and if we can get Grace there we can scare her into doing what we want."

"It's a possibility, but getting her to the stairs might be a problem. I suppose that she's in the Great Hall at the moment with all the other guests."

"Ah, that's where the cat can help us!"

"The cat! You've made friends with the ghost of a cat, or is it a real cat?"

"It's obviously a ghost because you couldn't see it when you nearly trod on it in the kitchen."

"OK, so how can a ghostly cat help get Grace out of the Great Hall?"

"Simple, we can tell Whiskers to steal something from Grace and run to the steps leading to the Clock Court, making sure Grace follows."

"Whiskers?"

"That's what she's called. I wanted to call her Snowy because she is all white but she said she had always been called Whiskers because she has long ones."

"Long what?"

"Whiskers, stupid!"

"You can talk to a cat and she can talk back to you?"

"Sort of. Anyway, have you a better plan?"

"Not really, but first we must say good bye to Charlotte, Jacob and Rebecca."

"I have introduced Charlotte and Jacob to Whiskers."

I groaned. "You've done what?"

"It was an accident really. We were playing a game of tag and Charlotte touched me just as Whiskers walked into the kitchen again."

"Did she scream?"

"No, not really. Of course she wanted to know why she could only see Whiskers when she was touching me. I tried to explain but I am not sure she understood. She's cool with it now and so is Jacob."

"Jacob knows about your powers of seeing ghosts? Anyone else?"

"Only Rebecca."

"Rebecca! Now we are in bother."

"No, we are not. I was able to get Rebecca to talk to Amy."

"Amy?"

"Her daughter who has just died. She is in limbo like Henry and Mary were."

Henry and Mary had been two ghosts that we had met on our first trip to the 17th century. It seemed, according to Eva, to be a place where those that have recently died wait before being called to their final resting place. The amount of time Eva could see them in 'Limbo' didn't seem consistent but had been a few weeks in the cases of Mary and Henry. The other places that Eva had been able to see her ghosts had been in what she described as the 'corridors of transit', which allowed some spirits to move to places of special meaning for them, such as the place where they were born or died. In the case of my grandmother Eva, from whom all this adventure had started, one such place was an old mission church she had attended throughout most of her life.

"Wasn't Rebecca scared by what you could do?"

"No. She believes in ghosts and had felt things in the Palace before."

"You mean the cat, Whiskers?"

"No. She thought that once she had met Queen Catherine in the Gallery. You know another of Henry VIII's wives. Apparently, the Gallery is the most haunted place in the Palace according to Rebecca."

"Perhaps we should have a word with Rebecca before we unleash Whiskers on poor Grace."

"Have you seen who's stood at the other end of the hall, John?"

I turned and there for a brief moment was the unmistakable figure of John Johnson, or Guy Fawkes as he is now better known.

"I wonder what he's doing in the Palace? Up to no good I should imagine," muttered Eva.
"He has probably been told to watch us. There are no mobile phones so how did Thomas get in touch with him?"
"He must have already been here, inside the Palace."

"I don't really trust that Guy and Thomas have our best interests at heart. I still think that it was Thomas who knocked me out."
"Let's go talk to Rebecca and the other lady, she seems nice."
"She's called Helen Little and she's the one that looks after King James' children. Very powerful lady so be careful what you say."
"Message understood!"

We headed back to the far end of the hall where Helen, Rebecca and the children stood. Helen spoke as we approached.
"Is everything alright? I do insist that we have someone to look at that head wound of yours before you leave the Palace."
"Yes please," I said, which seemed to surprise Eva.

"If you stay here I will send the physician to you. He shouldn't be long." She walked down the corridor and turned left to where we had seen Guy disappear.

"I am not sure I trust her," I whispered to Eva, "I think we need to leave before the so called physician arrives, he might be carrying more than a doctor's bag."

I turned to Rebecca. "Is there anywhere we can talk to you that is more private than in this hall?"
She thought for a moment and then said, "There is the bowling alley."

Eva and I looked at each other in amazement. "The Palace has a bowling alley?"
"Yes, King Henry had it built. In his younger days he was a great sportsman."

She too headed down the hall and turned left into the courtyard with the fountain in it and then straight on to the Clock Court. All four of us followed, although Charlotte and Jacob clearly knew where they were going. We went through another slightly larger courtyard until we arrived at a long narrow building. This was a bowling alley but not as Eva knew it.

"This isn't a bowling alley; it's just a long piece of grass."
"The skittles are at the other end somewhere and I guess Henry must have rolled balls down the grass."

"They don't even have gutters and one of those things that stops your ball from going in them. Where's the thing that returns the ball to you?"
"I think they might be called servants!"

Rebecca and the children clearly did not understand Eva's amazement at such a sparse 'bowling alley'.

"Look Rebecca, we need to talk to you about why we are here. I am sorry we had to involve you but we met Charlotte and Jacob outside the Palace and used the fact that your daughter Amy had died to gain entry to it. We are so sorry for you in losing your daughter."

"But Eva has shown me that Amy lives on and I have now met her once again which could not have happened without Eva's strange powers."
"And I saw Whiskers the cat," chimed in Jacob with some pride.

"The truth is that Thomas Percy has brought our friend Grace here to the Palace and she didn't want to come here. He forced her to come," Eva lied, "we need to get her away from him and back home with us."

The problem with 'back home' was that, in the short term at least, that was the house of Thomas and Martha Percy! I really didn't know what to say, but as ever, Eva did.

"I have a plan to get Grace out of the Great Hall so we can take her home."

"No Eva, I think that it's too dangerous to upset Thomas, perhaps the best plan is to go home and wait for Grace to arrive back."

"Maybe I could make a suggestion," said Rebecca. "Tomorrow the men are having a meeting about the new bible. The women are not invited to the meeting and so your Grace will be more easily spoken to with Thomas not being there."

"Do you know anything of a man called John Johnson, Rebecca?"
"No, why do you ask?"
"Because he is stood over there in the shadows watching us."

The instinct of the children was to turn around and see if they could see him, at which point the figure in the shadows disappeared.

"I can take you to a safe place where you can rest the night."
"That's a good idea. Thank you"

We followed Rebecca out of the bowling alley towards the kitchens and thankfully with no further sighting of Mr Johnson.

Two Queens of Hampton Court

According to Rebecca, everybody who had come for the conference was due to leave at the end of the week. I had lost track of days and dates, but it must have been nearly the end of March 1605, or maybe the beginning of April, quite a time still from the date that the famous 'plot' was due to take place.

She found us a small room quite close to the kitchen. It was clearly a storage area for pots and pans and it had a stone floor which was not the best sleeping surface for someone of my age. Rebecca, much to the disgust of her two children who would love to have had Eva for a 'sleep-over', had decided that it was too dangerous and difficult to let us sleep in the servants' quarters, so the 'pots and pans' room it was.

The room, being next to the kitchen, was quite warm, and with a blanket provided by Rebecca, Eva had no difficulty dropping off to sleep. After what seemed like hours I too must have fallen asleep.

I awoke some time later to the sound of Eva's voice whispering to someone but clearly not me. It was pitch black and I could not see Eva or whoever she was speaking to.

"Eva, what's wrong? Who are you speaking to?"
"Jane and Catherine!" came the reply.
"Who?"
"Shush!"
I did as I was told.

Some moments passed and all I think I heard were the words 'danger' and 'somebody in the kitchen' and a repetition of the two names, Jane and Catherine.

The whispering stopped and I felt a hand on the top my head. "There you are," she whispered, "Jane and Catherine say we have a problem. There's a man prowling around in the kitchen and he has a knife."

It was not the time to ask questions, I could hear noises in the kitchen. Maybe the time had come to render someone unconscious. There were plenty of utensils with which I could attempt to do it. I reasoned that while the door to our room was closed we were safe. As soon as it began to open I would strike with whatever came to hand!

Eva seemed very quiet and calm. Perhaps she, and her two friends, knew something I didn't. I felt around, trying not to be too vigorous in case I knocked something off the shelves. My hand touched something that was clearly metal of some description. It felt like a handle of some sort and I gripped it as tightly as I could.

Then it happened, the door swung open, creaking loudly and I struck. What I struck and where I struck I had no idea but I lashed out with whatever was in my hand and with as much power as I could. The second swing seemed to connect with something or someone and there followed a further sound of something hitting the ground. For a split second the thought uppermost in my mind was that I had hit Eva. I swung once more for good luck and seemed to hit something very solid and whatever was in my hand fell with a clatter. I stood for a moment waiting for something to happen.

"John! Are you alright?"
"Yes, and you?"
"I'm frightened. What has happened?"
"I don't know."

There was some dim light which seemed to come from two sources. One was the floor almost immediately in front of me and a glow from further back. With the door open that one must have been the embers of the kitchen fire, and the one on the floor suddenly became larger. Something had caught fire!

My instinct was to put the fire out, but as I moved towards it I tripped over something on the floor and fell headlong towards the flames. Putting my hands out instinctively to cushion my fall, I rolled on to my back, shaking my hands in a desperate attempt to put out any flames that had attached themselves to me.

As I sat up I could see Eva with a lighted taper in her hand and by its light I could see a heap of what looked like rags on the floor in front of me. I jumped up and stamped hard on the growing fire which seemed to be burning the rags. As I stamped down I heard a groan. With all but the smallest flames still flickering, I could see that the bundle of rags was actually the body of someone.

Suddenly Eva lashed out at the bundle of clothes with whatever she had in her hand. The bundle groaned and returned to a still position.
"Drag him to the fire, John, so we can see who it is!"
I think that we both knew who it was and if we had killed him we had just ruined the fun and excitement of millions of children for hundreds of years!

I pulled the unconscious body towards the fire and with some effort turned him onto his back. Eva was at my side with lighted taper still in hand.

"Where did you get that from?" I enquired.
"Jane gave me it. Apparently she carries it wherever she goes."

I let the explanation pass without comment and uncovered the face of our potential assailant. It was who we thought it was; Guy Fawkes!

"What are we going to do?" I asked Eva, looking for some of her usual inspiration.

"Catherine says we should kill him but I'm not sure that is a good idea. She is a very aggressive lady at present," Eva whispered.
"Could you introduce me to Jane and the aggressive Catherine?"
"Be careful, they are listening!"

I knew from past experience and the fact that there was no-one else around that Jane and Catherine must be the ghosts of the two Queens of England of whom she had spoken earlier.

"I thought you said that they stayed in the same place all the time."
"They were worried about me when they saw Mr Fawkes here and came to warn me."
"It's a good job they did. OK, I have never met a Queen before and now I am going to meet two; like London buses, you wait for ages and then two come at once!"
"I'll let you explain that comment to them."

Even in the dim glow of the fire, I could see that she had on one of her cheeky smiles. She reached over and touched me on the shoulder and, like all the other times she had done this, I could now see what she could see.

In front of me were two attractive ladies. On the left, dressed in a long white gown, was, I assumed, Jane Seymour as she didn't look aggressive at all; in fact she looked very angelic. On the right, also dressed in white but with long flowing hair and a look of despair on her face, was Catherine Howard. The difference in their demeanour was probably due to the fact that one had died and the other had been beheaded on the orders of her husband.

Catherine spoke first. "Do you know that Henry was out hunting when I was beheaded?"

Life never prepares you for questions like that! So in these circumstances meeting a question with a question is always a safe bet.

"What shall we do with this man?"
"Kill him!"
"No, Queen Catherine, that is not a good option, we need to keep him alive."
"He was trying to kill you and the young lady."
"That is true, but we are not violent people and don't want to do any further harm to him."

"We could take him to the fountain and awaken him. He might not remember what happened and think that he had drunk too much and fallen in the fountain," came a possible solution from Queen Jane.

"Why are you here?" Catherine said, "and why can you see us and talk to us, when nobody else can? We scare other people and they run away but you two are not scared."

"It's a long story. We are looking for a lady called Grace who is with Thomas Percy. We would like to take her home but Thomas won't let her go. This man Guy Fawkes works for Thomas and that is why he wants to get rid of us."

As Eva had said, Queen Jane was quite sympathetic and wanted to help the best she could. "Let us think about what to do. At least it is better than what we usually do and it is good to talk to you both, whatever the reasons are for being able to do so. Do you want Catherine and me to take this man to the fountain?"

"Can you do that?" exclaimed Eva.
"We have our ghostly ways Eva. You two try and go back to sleep and leave this horrid man to us."

"We ought to check that he is alright first. He is, in many ways, a very important person."
"Why is that, John?"
"It's difficult to explain but something he does in the future makes him very famous and if he was to die now the future would be changed for ever."
"Can you see into the future John?"

I looked at Eva for help and she smiled. She understood that the explanations to both the questions that the Queens had asked would come better from her and she could better explain the powers she had.

I moved away from Eva, losing both contact with her and the sight and sound of the two famous Queens. Eva started to explain our situation and I bent over the prone body of Guy Fawkes to see if he was ok. It was evident that I had caught him a nasty blow over his right eye. I could see a nasty gash with a fair amount of clotted blood over his face. I decided I needed to clean up the wound and wait until he regained consciousness before we could move him to a fountain, or anywhere else for that matter.

I noticed that there was some form of lamp lying on the floor. It must have been the candle from that lamp which had started the small fire that I had inadvertently fallen into. It was at that moment that I felt the pain from the burn on my right hand which probably a little water would relieve. When I was younger we had always regarded our own spit as being a good antiseptic for things like stings and burns. Whether it was an old wives' tale or not I don't know, but I spat on my hand. It seemed to help. Just beyond the lamp I could see another object on the floor. It was a knife and a chilling thought went through my mind that it was with that weapon that Guy Fawkes had intended to kill both Eva and me.

Clearly, for some reason I did not understand at the moment, Thomas Percy wanted Eva and me dead and was willing to instruct someone else to carry it out. Maybe Grace had said something silly about us knowing about the 'Gunpowder Plot', as it was to become known. I suppose they would have referred to it then as an assassination attempt on King James I. At that moment I decided, as the saying goes, 'keep your friends close but keep your enemies closer', that it would be better to keep Guy with us and show a bit of human kindness. I knew he was Spanish but assumed that his level of knowledge of the English language would be good, since he had attended St Peter's School in York.

I picked up the knife and looked around in the dim light for any cord that I might use to restrict Guy's movement. Eva was still talking to Jane and Catherine and I asked her to ask them to see if they could help with Guy's wound and maybe find a place where we could hide him for the time being; and we also needed something to restrain him with!

I got the usual look from Eva because, yet again, I had forgotten that because I couldn't see or hear the ghosts it didn't mean they couldn't see or hear me.

One of the two Queens must have explained where we could find water and the necessary cord and even suggested a good hiding place for Guy. But I really wanted to talk to him before any of the aggressive stuff started and wished he would return to consciousness.

There was no chance that we could go back to sleep but being here beside the fire was as good a place as any to stay the rest of the night until Guy awoke and the kitchen staff arrived.

According to Eva, the Queens had left in search of the required items.

"They are being very helpful," I said.

"I think that they are curious about us. Their world is restricted in the main to this Palace whereas we can travel both through England and time!"

Jon Stow

With the aid of Rebecca, Charlotte, Jacob and the two Queens of England we ducked and dived out of people's way at the Palace until the end of the week was nearly upon us. The plan that Eva and Queen Jane had devised for the capture of Grace seemed to be based loosely on the fact that it would be easier to do it as she left the conference. In truth, they hadn't let me in on the finer details of the plan but having seen Eva at work before, when she put a large Civil War cannon out of action almost single handedly, she was well capable of a simple kidnap, particularly with Queen Jane as an ally. The conference, I learned, was due to finish on the 5th April. We really could do with being on our way to Great Staughton to complete the return of Valentine well before the sparks began to fly, literally or not, on the 5th November. The ideal situation would have been to take Grace out of the grasp of Thomas, get back to Westminster, pick up Valentine from Martha and leave London as soon as possible.

Oh, if only things could be that easy?

Reluctantly the bound Guy Fawkes had briefly spoken to Eva and me. The situation seemed quite surreal. Here was the man whose effigy had helped us raise money for fireworks which we then used to celebrate his death and burn the effigy of him on a bonfire! He did confess to wanting us dead but was reluctant to tell us why Thomas wanted us dead, or even that it was Thomas that had put him up to it. I made a pathetic attempt to try and frighten him into telling us more but even my impression of bad cop, Gene Hunt from 'Life on Mars', didn't have much effect. However, as always, Eva had a trick up her sleeve that really unhinged the arrogant Guy. I wasn't present at the time and have only Eva's recollection of the event to relate.

She had gone to feed Guy some manchet that we had stolen. Jane had found an ideal place to hide the prisoner and unbeknown to poor Guy he was being guarded by Catherine 24:7. We had cleaned up his wound and for that he should have been grateful but as ever he wasn't a happy bunny. He had made some attempts to talk Eva into untying him but he had more chance of knitting fog!

On this particular occasion, according to Eva, he was particularly arrogant and angry that he should be the prisoner of a little girl. Calling Eva 'a little girl' was not a smart move and probably was the last straw leading to what she did next.

She had asked him a number of times about why Thomas wanted us dead. On this occasion, he was scornful once again and swore at her. She gently touched him on the shoulder and showed him a world he had never seen before. The world of a large phantom dog that Eva had met on her travels around the Palace. By all accounts it was an evil-looking beast in the mould of the Hound of the Baskervilles of Sherlock Holmes fame. Its mouth slavered white foam and it made sounds which sent shivers up most living people's spine and poor Guy was no exception. He screamed which would have been a problem if the room Jane had selected for him hadn't been in one of the most secret inaccessible places in the Palace. It was in one of the underground tunnels which ran from the Palace towards the River Thames.

She had released him from her touch so that he could recover but threatened him again with the hound of death. She summoned the hound several times. Eventually he succumbed and told us that it was because we wanted to take Grace away that Thomas had ordered our deaths! No mention of any plot being discovered. It was simply a selfish wish to keep a beautiful young girl to himself that had made him command Guy to kill us. The thought that both these men would be dead in seven months wasn't so callous anymore.

Although we both wanted to, we couldn't leave Guy Fawkes in his prison for ever. He was too important to history and we could not interfere with what was to be his destiny. We had to release him or at least let someone know where he was being imprisoned.

Rebecca was being a real superstar, although it was not a word she would have recognized. She organized the theft of things for Guy and ourselves to eat and drink. But of all the things she did for us, the washing of our over-used clothes was the most appreciated. Wearing the same set of clothes over a period of time meant, to put it bluntly, we smelt!

As mentioned previously, Rebecca's husband had died of the plague a year or so ago but she had not yet got around to throwing all his clothes away, partly because she said that they might still be infected. This I doubted and I was more than willing to wear the 'new' clothes that she offered. It seemed reasonable that any infection that had been on them would have died by now, but what did I know? Anyway, I took a risk and tried them on. They weren't a bad fit. He must have been a little taller than me as the sleeves and trouser legs were a little too long. However I was more than delighted to get out of my smelly clothes provided initially by Henry Pickering.

Eva was less fortunate. She was too big for Charlotte's clothes, even if she had a spare set, but she did just squeeze into Amy's clothes. She had the same reluctance to get into a dead person's clothes as I had but the way she smelt was key in her decision to do it. Washing in cold water was also something difficult to get used to. Oh, for a hot bath or shower.

I was standing, having one of these cold washes, stripped to the waist, when Eva burst in without an apology.

"They've gone!"

"Who has?"

"Grace and Thomas!"

"What!"

"Jane says that they went late last night and there was nothing she could do about it."

"But they were supposed to leave today. The conference doesn't end until today!"

"They have gone! What shall we do?"

I thought for a moment. "We need to take a look at that history book you brought to find out exactly what is going to happen to Thomas. Where is it now?"

As I mentioned earlier, this history book about the 17th century that I had bought in a hurry in a shop in Castleford, had helped on our first visit, particularly in knowing what was going to happen at the Battle of Edgehill.

"It's still in the rucksack back at Thomas' and Martha's house in Westminster. I should have brought it with me, I know!"

"Not to worry. We have to go back there now so we can read up on what happens to Thomas."

"Why does knowing what happens to Thomas, help us to find Grace?

"It might tell us where Thomas Percy goes after the 'Gunpowder Plot' fails."

"Still don't understand why that would be of any use to us."

"Well, perhaps we could go there and wait for him, and hope and pray he brings Grace with him."

"That's not a bad idea John! For you!"

"Thanks," but I wasn't sure it was such a good idea. Anything might happen to Grace between now and 5th November.

"What do you think we should do now?"

"I don't think Thomas and Grace will go back to the Westminster house, because John and Martha are not too pleased with them. If we could get back there and collect the book and our things . . ."

"And Valentine!"

"Oh yes, I forgot poor Valentine. With all the problems we have had with Grace I had forgotten the real reason for us being here. Maybe we should just leave Grace to whatever befalls her. It's her stupid fault anyway."

"That's not strictly true, John. It was my fault for dragging her with you into Henry's 'corridor of transit'. Remember?"

"Yes, I suppose you are right and we ought to try and get her back home safe and sound too."

"What do you think we should do next?"

"Well, pick up Valentine and our belongings from the house in Westminster, have a look at the book to see if it says anything about where Thomas finishes up after the 'Gunpowder Plot' fails, then make our way there and wait for him to arrive. Hopefully he brings Grace with him and we collect her and get on our way to Great Staughton and drop Valentine off with his mother . . ."

"And hopefully go home! Simple!" Eva completed the perfect scenario.

"That's the plan!"

Well, it seemed straightforward enough but there were a few 'ifs' and 'maybes' and I think we both realized that things might not go to plan, but at least it was a plan.

At that moment Rebecca, Charlotte and Jacob entered the room.

"Oh sorry!" exclaimed Rebecca, and I then realized that I was still half naked. I grabbed the shirt she had given me and made myself decent by 17th century standards. In 2008 nobody would have blinked an eyelid, never mind apologized.

Rebecca blushed a little and apologized again.

When she had recovered a little she said, "Can I talk to you John?"

"Yes of course."

She hesitated.

"You can speak in front of Eva, Rebecca, we have no secrets."

"I have been talking to Charlotte . . . ."

"And me!" piped in Jacob.

"Oh and Jacob of course. There is nothing left for us here at the Palace with my eldest daughter and husband dead. I hate London and the death it brings. We would like to come with you. The children get on so well with Eva. I have never seen them so happy as when they play with her."

I could only guess at what Eva had done with Charlotte and Jacob to make them so happy. But she had a natural way with children and brought out the best in them. Her special powers helped I suppose. It brought the children into a world that only dreams or nightmares are made of!

Before I could speak, Eva beat me to it.
"We would love you to come with us, but it might be dangerous. You know that there are people out there who want to kill us."
"Why is that?"

Eva and I looked at each other. Should we try and explain? Would Rebecca believe what we told her? Eva had helped her to see her dead daughter Amy for one more time so maybe she could believe the impossible. I nodded at Eva.

She spoke slowly.
"Er . . . John is my grandfather and we come from the future, from the year 2008 to be precise. As you know Rebecca, I have special powers and we came to this century some years ago to reunite a father and his son. Things went wrong and we took the child back to our time. We have now come back to these times in order to reunite him with his mother."

This was as good a short summary as could be given.

"What happened to the child's father?"
"He died at the battle of Marston Moor in the Civil War," Eva said with a clarity of memory which belied her years.
"What was the Civil War?"

This was a more difficult question to answer!
"King James' son Charles becomes king . . .
"What happened to the lovely Prince Henry? Prince Charles is too weak a child to become king. He stammers so and the tantrums he has! They would test a saint."

This was getting a little stressful for both Eva and Rebecca.
"I am sorry," said Eva, "but Henry dies of a fever at the age of eighteen."
Wow, what a memory! Although I wasn't absolutely certain that a fever was the full cause of his death.

"Anyway," Eva continued, "Charles has an argument with Parliament and a war starts between those who support the King and those who support Parliament. Lots of people are killed."

Rebecca looked dreadful. She was a sensitive woman and clearly all this information about death was too much for her and she burst into tears. I had no choice but to put my arm around her in an attempt to comfort her. Even Charlotte and little Jacob, who probably did not understand what Eva had said, began to cry at their mother's distress.

"I think that's enough information for now Eva."

"Sorry I was only . . . ."

"Yes, I know. You were answering her questions and maybe later you can tell her more."

I turned to Rebecca and probably mistakenly said, "It would be good if you came with us because Charlotte and Jacob would be good company for Eva and you can help us with your knowledge of London and these strange times that we know very little about."

She smiled and seemed pleased with the decision to let her and her children go with us.

"What do you plan to do?"

"Now we have lost our friend Grace, we need to return to Thomas Percy's house in Westminster and collect Valentine, the child we are returning to his mother, and all our belongings and leave London before Thomas finds us."

"Won't Thomas go back to his house?"

"I doubt it. He has been away with another woman and his wife knows and isn't too pleased about the situation. He may hide for a time."

There were lots of people leaving Hampton Court on the 6th April and this made it easier for the five of us to leave with them. Most of the people leaving had attended the conference which we gathered was something to do with the New King James Bible as it came to be known. Probably at that time it had no such grand title and was in modern day speak, 'an opening up of dialogue' between powerful and interested parties of the time.

It was what could be described as a crisp spring morning when we passed under the arch at the end of the final courtyard of Hampton Palace, leaving by, what Rebecca called, the West exit. We didn't have the money to hire a carriage, although there were lots of them about, picking up all the really important people. Some would have been privately-owned carriages with servants at the reins, but it was clear that a number of private enterprises of the time were plying their trade and trying to find customers requiring lifts into the City of London.

We walked along the river bank although I didn't have the confidence that Rebecca could direct us the fourteen or so miles back to the house in Westminster. The journey should have been about six and a half hours walking at the pace young Jacob was doing. It seemed unfair to make a boy so young walk all that way, but he didn't complain and trudged onward.

After about an hour and a half we stopped to let Jacob and Charlotte, and in truth me, get a rest. We sat down by the banks of the River Thames and Rebecca delved into the bag that she had been carrying and brought out some manchet. She had managed to purloin some of the bread-like substance and some weak beer which she had given me to carry in a sort of pot jar. It had been this that had really tired me out because it was not light! And I wasn't getting any younger or fitter.

It was a welcome rest and a meal in pleasant circumstances.

"Can you see that strange man over there? He has been watching us for quite a time. I wonder if he is one of Thomas Percy's men who is tailing us," said Eva, as we had just about finished our meal and were making plans to move on.

"I cannot see any such man. Where exactly are you looking?"
"Can you see the big tree, which has two smaller ones either side of it?"
"Yes"
"Well, the man is stood at the base of the tree on the right. See him?"
"No, I can't see any such man."

"OK I'll be back in a minute," she said and walked off in the direction of the large tree. She seemed to make a detour around the tree and came back to the smaller one on the right. I assumed that if he was watching us she had approached him from behind. She stood there for a time and then started talking. Modern-day people would have assumed that she was on a hands-free mobile phone. To 17th century people she would appear to be a mad woman talking to herself. Rebecca and the children were also watching her.

"What is Eva doing, John?" said Charlotte.

I thought for a moment. What could I say, but I was certain Charlotte knew enough about Eva's powers to understand the truth.

"She is talking to the ghost of a man who has probably just died."

"How do you know he has just died?" Rebecca was inquisitive.

"Well it appears from Eva's previous meetings with ghosts that there are two types of situations. Firstly that the ghost haunts the place where they were born or the place where they died or some other special place. They seem to be allowed three options once they have been through Limbo."

"Is that a place?" said Rebecca

"No, it appears that for a period of time after someone dies they can move around in Limbo until a decision about their final resting place is made and then they disappear. Seems strange, I know, but we first met our friend Henry Pickering when he had just been killed and was in Limbo. He helped us through some pretty tricky times."

"You do have a funny way of talking John. 'Pretty tricky'? I have never heard that expression before."

"Sorry. He helped us through a difficult time in the Civil War,"

"I hope I am not around when that happens. When does it start?"

"About 1642. The first major battle is near Banbury in September of that year."

"I will be quite old by then, but sadly the children won't be. Can you look after them for me John?"

"I don't know where I will be when it starts. I have seen it once and am not too keen on seeing it again."

"Couldn't you take Charlotte and Jacob back with you to 2008?"

"You don't really mean that do you?"

"From what Eva has told me and the children, it is a very exciting time with . . . what did Eva call those things . . . . ?"

"Commuters," piped in Jacob yet again. Both he and Charlotte had been listening intently to our conversation.

"Not quite right Jacob. I think that she may have told you about computers."

"That's right and they have nets and webs and can catch a virus like the plague!"

"And you have to kick them with your boots when they die!"

"Perhaps we can talk about this later. Look, Eva is coming back."

"Who is he?" I said as Eva approached.

"He is a very nice man and wants to help us. His name is Jon Stow and dying has come as a bit of a shock to him even though he is quite old."

Didn't dying come as a shock to most people?

"Jon Stow!" exclaimed Rebecca. "He is a very clever man. He carried out a survey of all the streets of London and had a plan published a few years ago."

I resisted the temptation to say, 'was a very clever man'.

"Come and talk to him," said Eva.

We all walked the short distance to the tree where apparently Jon Stow stood, although none of us with the exception of Eva could, as yet, see him. Both Charlotte and Jacob were clear on what they must do to see ghosts, whereas their mother was a little unsure. To any onlookers it must have been a strange sight. Eva held Charlotte by the hand, whilst Charlotte held Jacob's hand. I encouraged Rebecca to touch Eva's right shoulder whilst I was on the left. From Mr. Stow's position it must have looked like one of those very posed photographs that families do in a studio!

Anyway, in this formation we could all get a good look at Mr. Jon Stow. He was tall and very lean both in his body and in his face. He had very small eyes through which he smiled at the assembled audience and began to speak slowly.

Sadly, it transpired that Jon Stow had died that very day, 6th April 1605 and that he was nearly 80 years old. He had indeed mapped the streets of the City of London which he proudly stated had been published in 1598 in the reign of Elizabeth I. He was a great friend of Ben Jonson who was, according to Jon, a great poet and actor. I suspect that the children were less impressed by this rendition than they were of the fact that they were listening to a dead man speak!

Despite his achievements, he had died a very poor man, although 'good King James' had tried to raise money through 'kind gratuities' and other donations from the people of London. Despite his apparent demise he seemed a very cheerful and upbeat sort of a person.

From what I understood of his explanation, he was the son of Thomas Stow, a tallow-chandler making candles. He had been born in 1525 and although he did not follow his father's trade, had been apprenticed as a merchant tailor, being admitted to the Merchant Taylor's company in the late 1540s and then he had established a business at a house near Aldgate, between Leadenhall and Fenchurch Street. He obviously liked to talk, or was it the fact that in the very short time he had been dead, he had had little chance to meet and talk to anyone!

Eva had obviously explained some of our plight and the good Jon Stow had volunteered to help in a number of ways. Firstly he had a plan or map to help us on our way back to Westminster and he had some money with which we could buy food and drink. But most importantly he possessed a small horse and cart which we could use to speed up our journey. Perfect, except we had to walk to Jon's house and convince his widow that he wanted us to have all of the afore-mentioned items!

I had a bit of a bad feeling about this. The good Mrs Stow might not be so amenable given that she had, that very day, lost her husband. Anyway it was worth a try in order to speed up our journey to Westminster. With Eva's powers we could convince her that the taking of the map, the money and the horse and cart were all the idea of her dear beloved departed husband!

Westminster again

We walked further along the banks of the River Thames. The river was both a depository for all types of refuse of the very worst kind and a source of water supply! No wonder disease was rife in the City of London. Miles and miles of the River Thames, running as it did from the west before it even got to the City of London, was awash with the filth and garbage of thousands of people. Jon had said in one of his many discourses that the population of London at that time was 'a vast total' of 200,000; and the pollution that all that number of people made was destined to end up in the River Thames. I felt like telling him that the population was now about eight million and the pollution problems were just as bad in London but not quite in the same way since fish could be actually found swimming in the River Thames!

We left it to Eva to tell us where Jon was going. We moved away from the river and into some rows of houses. The big difference in the streets of London then and now was not just in the materials of which the houses were made or the horrible pollution which was evident in the street, but the individuality of the houses. The estates, if that's what you could call them, were made from quite distinctly shaped houses, not the uniform shapes of 20th and 21st centuries.

We turned into Lime Street where apparently Jon had lived for most of his life after moving from Threadneedle Street. It was a simple house without the grandeur of Thomas Percy's house. Jon and Eva had come up with a plan so as not to scare his lovely wife, Anne.

Apparently, Jon Stow had twice been brought under suspicion during the reign of Elizabeth for having Catholic sympathies. His house had been searched twice and some of his books confiscated as being 'dangerous and superstitious' and 'in defence of papistry'. However, he had been able to convince his interrogators that he was a good Protestant. He said that his reason for saying all this to Eva was the fact that Anne would be very frightened of people coming to the house and making enquiries.

The plan was simple! To let Anne talk to Jon once again. OK it would be scary to start with and have to be engineered by getting Anne to touch Eva but it was the best plan to convince her we meant her no harm.
Eva and I, with Rebecca, Charlotte and Jacob bringing up the rear, approached the door. The house did look as if there was no-one at home. My first rap at

the door went unanswered but the second brought movement from within the house. The door was opened slowly and suspiciously. There stood a frail old lady, certainly well into her 70s, dressed top to toe in black, looking every inch the grieving widow.
"How can I help you? It is not a good time for visitors."

I started my rehearsed lines.
"We would like to offer our sympathy at the sad passing of your husband. He was such a lovely man and did great things for the City of London. We would like to pay our respects to him."

Anne clearly looked shocked at what I had said.
"But . . . ." she stammered. "He has only just passed away and I have told no-one apart from the doctor and priest who were here to witness his passing. I have only just had time to change into my mourning clothes and you appear!"

She was getting upset and I found myself lost for words. The rest of what I rehearsed didn't seem appropriate.
Eva stepped forward and simply said "May we come inside and explain?"
Anne hesitated for a moment and then moved back without saying a word. Eva moved passed her and the rest of us followed.

Eva continued. "Please sit down Mrs Stow. I have something to show you, but first I must explain."
Anne dutifully sat down, still in a little shock at the turn of events but, I felt, not as shocked as she would be in

a few minutes after Eva had performed what she had done many times over.

Considering that there were six, maybe even seven people in the room (I had no idea where Jon was) you could have heard the proverbial pin drop. Charlotte and Jacob were remarkably well-behaved for ones so young in strange circumstances and seemed to sense the gravity of what was about to happen, maybe because they themselves had had such a moment when Eva introduced them to their recently deceased sister, Amy.

Eva started, as she often did, in a quiet methodical way to explain the powers that she had before she demonstrated them. She told Anne about meeting Jon this morning by the banks of the River Thames and the suggestion that he had made in order to help us return to Westminster. Nothing was said about our circumstances or why the journey was necessary, merely that Jon in his natural helpful way, even in death, had offered us help with money to buy food and transport to make our journey shorter.

Anne displayed the kind of belief in Eva's story that anyone being asked by complete strangers to relinquish money and the family horse and trap would do, but before she could utter the words to ask us to leave her in peace, Eva reached over and took Anne by the hand and gestured towards the door through which we had just entered. None of us, of course, could see what she could see but what was apparent was the look of shock that now covered her face. She screamed!

"Jon, my darling, my darling," and she rushed towards the door losing contact with Eva and then stopped dead in her tracks as she lost sight of her husband. She swung back to face Eva, looking wildly around the room.

"He's gone! He was over there and now he's gone!" she repeated.
"Come and sit down," Eva said quietly and calmly, "Let me explain."

Reluctantly, Anne returned to her seat, looking bewildered as anyone would.
"I don't understand. Where did he go?"
"He is still there but you don't have the powers to see him. Once you lost contact with me, he disappeared from your view."

"Who are you? Catholics? The King's interrogators?"
"No, we do not come from the King or from anyone who wishes you harm. Perhaps it is best if I let Jon explain. Please hold my hand again and try to be calm. Jon will talk to you about us."

It was clear to me that Eva was getting some kind of commentary from Jon as to what was the best approach to take with Anne.

Anne slowly rose from the chair and took hold of the hand that Eva offered her. There then began a conversation between Anne and Jon, of which most of us in the room could only hear one side, since we were not in contact with Eva and couldn't hear or see Jon.

Jon must have explained to Anne a little of what had happened that morning and that it had given him the chance to talk her.

Anne's responses were questioning and to the point.
"You want me to do what?"
"Money and a plan of the City?"
"The horse and trap? Are you sure? Do you know these people?"

Eventually, after several more questions and their silent replies, Anne turned to Eva and said, "If Jon is coming with you to Westminster then I want to come too."

This was news to the rest of us since we had no knowledge that Jon was going anywhere with us but it was obviously part of the bargaining that had gone on between husband and wife.

"I am going to change my clothing. I do not want to travel to Westminster dressed like this," Anne said in a very emphatic manner as if that was the final word on the matter and she disappeared to change.

Eva explained that Jon had suggested that, if Anne was unsure, she should take the money with her for the food they might need and drive the horse and trap to Westminster and thus be able to return in it after dropping us off at Thomas Percy's house. This compromise, although meaning quite a bit of travel for Anne, had allayed her fears that somehow we were trying to trick her out of money and goods. I failed to see how we could have performed any such illusion with mirrors or otherwise but at least the compromise would save us time and effort in getting back to Westminster and allow Anne some extra time with her newly-deceased husband.

Anne arrived suitably dressed for the journey and asked us to follow her to where the horse and trap were housed. Fortunately, it was quite a big carriage. Anne insisted on 'driving' provided Eva sat next to her so she could see and speak to Jon. Obviously, she wished to get as much contact with Jon as possible even if it was only with his ghost. Eva held the map by which Anne and presumably Jon navigated the streets of London heading for Westminster.

In the back sat Rebecca and her two children and of course yours truly. The cobbled streets did not make for a comfortable journey but it was far better than walking. The conversation in the front seemed to be a typical one between a long-time married couple and the art of finding the best route with the aid of a map. Sadly no sat-nav! I really don't know what Jon and Anne would have made of that device. I once read a book that my wife, also called Ann but without the 'e', gave me which was entitled 'Why women cannot read maps and men never ask for directions'. An interesting book although I felt it unwise to mention it in the present situation. There were four women in the carriage and two of them were trying to read the map created by the man who sat alongside them!

Two strange thoughts popped into my mind. Firstly that my wife was by common consent a better driver than I was but not quite such a good navigator and secondly the sort of things she would say when we got lost like 'how did we get to there on the map?' and the equally baffling 'we seem to have lost Ghent' which would have come as quite a shock to the people of that large Belgian city.

There certainly seemed to be an equally bizarre conversation going on up front where Eva seemed to be acting as peacemaker. Anne seemed to have forgotten that her husband had sadly died this morning and they were back to the old ways of having a good disagreement!

"We've never travelled in a carriage before have we, Ma?" Jacob broke the silence in the back row.
"No, I don't think you have. I did once when I was a small girl."
"It's nice to wave to people as we pass." It was nice to see the age-old tradition of children waving from moving vehicles whether they be trains, boats or carriages.

We had one stop for refreshments and a toilet break which I will not dwell on except to say there were no 'rest rooms' available or roadside service stations.

We continued our journey with few problems except Eva relaxed a little too much and turned to me and said "Isn't it good to be on a road with no cars or traffic lights?"

Rebecca gave me a quizzical look and Anne just stared at Eva as if she was mad, but it was left to good old Jacob to ask the obvious.

"What are cars, Eva? I've never heard of them."
There was a moment's silence as Eva prepared what was going to be an interesting answer.
"No, Jacob, I said cows. Where I come from in the countryside we get a lot of cows that walk into the way of carriages as they are being moved from one place to another.

What a genius! Go on Jacob, I thought, ask her about the traffic lights, but he never did and all went silent.

Anne seemed keen to tell us about the changes that she had seen in the City of London and its surrounding countryside. She talked about the time she had spent in the small village of Charing where the famous Charing Cross was situated. How Hampstead Heath was a desolate moor and had become a haunt for criminals, who could hide in the surrounding forest of Middlesex. Cattle and sheep were pastured at Islington then herded for slaughter at Smithfield. The corn for London's bread was now ground in windmills at Finsbury, Islington, Lambeth and Greenwich. She was the proverbial mine of useless information but Eva listened intently as she continued her monologue.

"Shame that St Paul's spire burnt down a few years back, it was such a landmark. I remember being about thirty years old when it went up in flames. I suppose the Royal Exchange between Cornhill and Threadneedle Street, which was built just after, is a bit of a landmark now. It has about a hundred shops on the first floor above the colonnade, and the turreted Nonsuch House was, they say, built in Holland and brought over and erected on London Bridge. That bridge is too narrow. With all the carts and drays and the increase in those infernal Hackney coaches and Sedan chairs that use it, it's really hazardous. There have been deaths on that bridge".

I, and I expect Eva, had no idea what a colonnade was or why a house should be called Nonsuch, but in a way it passed the time and kept Anne happy as she carefully manoeuvred the carriage around slower-moving traffic. I wish I could have transported Anne, there and then into 21st century London with its traffic jams and road works and see what she thought of that!

The shops we passed were no more than stalls or sheds. Signs swung in the wind. Although some houses were made of brick, most buildings had wooden frames. Often the upper floors would jut out from the front, so they overhung the street below. It reminded me of the Shambles, that famous street in the City of York. There weren't as many thatched roofs as I had expected and I was surprised to see so many roofs made from tiles and lead. As we neared the City of London the pollution of smoke from coal fires increased, the smoke being taken up and out of the houses through a chimney causing patches of fog to form.

The streets really did begin to smell. Piles of rubbish were just left in the streets and according to Anne, they were left to be picked up each night by 'rakers', whom she thought did not do as good a job as she would have liked. The smelly human waste that was put in cesspits that lined the road were apparently also emptied every night, but that was hard to believe. Many of the gutters were blocked and the dirty water sometimes seemed to be flooding back into the houses nearby. I could see clothes being washed in the already dirty River Thames which smelt of mud and slime and I saw several dead dogs lying by the side of the road.

I don't know if Anne was joking but apparently that's exactly how Houndsditch got its name! Dead dogs in ditches!

With all these insanitary conditions, it was easy to see how plagues could spread, causing death and destruction.

I was certainly pleased when we arrived safely at the house of Thomas Percy in Westminster.

Westward ho!

Martha looked pleased to see us. Whether that was because she had had to cope with Valentine for longer than she had expected or that she wanted news of what had happened to her husband, I am not sure. We introduced Anne Stow, Rebecca and her two children to Martha but for obvious reasons we left out Jon. We told her of our news from Hampton Court, including the fact that we had no idea of where her husband was, but that he was probably still with Grace. We thanked her for all the help she had given us and we would pick up our belongings and be leaving that day. She asked where we were heading and since we had not had time to read the book yet, Eva just replied vaguely that we had to take Valentine back to his mother.

Leaving Martha and Anne talking in the hallway, Eva and I returned to our rooms and picked up what meagre belongings we had, but most importantly the book. Eva brought it into my room and quite surprisingly handed it to me.

The book had a number of references to 'Percy, Thomas'; two of which were on pages 36 and 37. I quickly turned to page 36. It was a general reference to the plotters focussing more on the plight of Sir Thomas Tresham who had, as a loyal Catholic, spent some time in prison. The paragraph ended:-

'Even before the gunpowder plotters had designed their own coup, at least two violent plots had been exposed in 1604, one meaning to abduct the King and hold him hostage until parliament agreed to demands to tolerate Catholicism in England. But the plan launched by Robert Catesby together with Tresham's son, Francis, Sir Everard Digby, Thomas Percy, Thomas Winter, and Guido Fawkes, a soldier who had served the Spanish armies in the Netherlands, and blessed by a Jesuit, Father Thomas Garnet, was much more dramatic.'

This was not what we wanted but after a description of what the plot entailed and how it failed came the information we required on page 37.

"Listen, this is it! 'A search was made of the cellars beneath the Westminster house whose premises had been rented by Thomas Percy. There they found Fawkes together with thirty-six barrels of gunpowder, enough to destroy the entire House of Lords immediately above the cellar. The confederates came to famously gruesome ends; Catesby and

Thomas Percy were tracked down to their safe house, called Holbeche House in Staffordshire which was owned by Stephen Littleton, and killed in the assault.' That's where we are heading, Holbeche House in Staffordshire."

I opted not to tell Eva about the gruesome details of Catesby's and Percy's deaths even though she might yet see it at first hand.

"Where in Staffordshire is Holbeche House?" asked Eva.
"It doesn't say but maybe Martha will know where it is and how to get there."
"I told her we were going to take Valentine home."
"OK, we have to be a bit more underhand then!"

We had a last minute look around our rooms, as everybody does when they leave a room for the final time; under the bed, in the drawers etc, a real ritual with my wife and me as we left any hotel room that we had stayed in.

We joined Martha and Anne still talking in the hallway in which we had left them.
"I don't suppose you know Stephen Littleton, do you Martha?"
"Why yes, I know him well. Why do you ask?"
"He is a friend of a friend of mine, and after we have taken Valentine home, we would like to visit him." Well, if Stephen was Thomas' friend, this was sort of true, although whether I would have called Thomas a friend is debatable.

"He lives in Holbeche House which is in the village of Kingswinford which is near Warwick. It is a fair way to travel but if you have a carriage?"

I looked at Anne and she smiled, surprising since her tour of duty had just ended.
"Can we take Jon there?" she asked.
Martha looked slightly puzzled.
"Yes of course we can," said Eva sympathetically.

We said our sad good-byes to Martha. Unlike her husband, she had been very kind to us all and in difficult circumstances. After all, we had brought the woman who had run off with her husband! We once again clambered into our positions in the carriage, and when Martha was out of sight, Anne said what she had wanted to say for some time.

"Now where are we going? This is fun!"
"I am hungry," said Jacob.
"Me too!" chimed in Charlotte.
"And me!" agreed Eva.
"OK, we will have a little to eat and discuss what we are going to do next."

We found a suitable place to eat the last of what Anne and Rebecca had brought with them and a discussion took place as to our plans. Eva and I couldn't be too specific about what we wanted to do as it involved the 'Gunpowder Plot' and that hadn't happened yet. Anne seemed to have forgotten that in her room at home she had the potentially decaying remains of her dear departed husband, with whom, with Eva's help, she was now in deep conversation.

"Jon and I think that we would like to help you all a little more. It's exciting and Jon and I are having more time together than would normally be possible."

That was undeniably true. I looked at Eva for some assistance and as usual she was forthcoming.
"What we are doing is very dangerous. Someone is trying to kill us and they have already tried to do so."
"That is not a problem to Jon, he is already dead and I like an adventure. At my time of life there isn't too much excitement."

Eva tried again. "If our past experiences are anything to go on, Jon will not be around for too long and that will leave you miles away from home, with his funeral still to arrange."

There was a brief one-sided conversation between Jon and Anne and then she said, "Can we at least take you back to our house? It's on your way out of London and towards Warwick where your friend lives. We could give you some money and food, and Jon says that you can have the carriage as I no longer have the use for it."

"That's very kind of you both. Are you sure that you want to do all that at this difficult time for you both?"
"Yes we do! It's decided. Westward ho and back home we go!" she shouted.

All of us had to smile at the sheer enthusiasm of Anne for the task in hand.

"Westward ho!" shouted Jacob and Charlotte in unison.

I touched Eva gently on the shoulder, not to view Jon but to whisper, "Let me know when Jon disappears."

"OK," she quietly replied.

The journey back to where Jon and Anne lived was uneventful but pleasant. The navigation was a little less fraught and the chatter both at the front of the carriage and the back was light-hearted.

In the front the discussion between Jon and Anne, via Eva of course, was still with regard to the way that London was deteriorating with its pollution, fog and criminal gangs, whilst Jacob and Charlotte were playing some sort of game invented by themselves. Rebecca and I just smiled as the pair seemed to argue about the rules governing the game. It did have a secondary use in that it kept Valentine amused. He had such a happy demeanour but from time to time he would cry as if to say I am fed up with this bumpy ride and console himself by sucking his left thumb. I had no idea how all this chopping and changing of people and places would affect his personality and long-term development. I had not, as yet, had to cater for his more basic needs and was really pleased that Rebecca was around to help. Was it Piaget who said 'show me the child at seven years old and I will show you the man'? He might have had a difficulty with this young time-traveller!

Eventually the tiring day was beginning to have an effect on all of the children, including Eva, as it was getting quite late. Charlotte and Jacob snuggled down at the side of their mother as the light began to fade and Valentine quickly fell asleep in my arms. Anne's job of guiding a tiring horse became more difficult, what with the gloom and difficult road surfaces together with the fact that Eva's head now rested on her shoulder. This had benefits for Anne who could see and talk to Jon without any extra assistance. As to whether Jon enjoyed the conversations I had no idea.

Eventually we arrived back at Jon's and Anne's house. With hardly any house or street lights and only the light of the moon for guidance, the last half an hour became very tricky. Anne feared for us, as at any moment a gang of thieves might suddenly attack a slow-moving vehicle such as ours.

The sleeping arrangements were a little ad hoc as Anne thought Rebecca and I were married. We compromised and I slept on the floor of the 'guest' bedroom with Valentine in the bed next to Rebecca. The other three children slept downstairs.

It was a very comfortable and, as one might expect, an 'oldie worldie' type of house with a few books and ornaments around. These artefacts marked the house out as belonging to a learned couple and they would have made quite a profit on the television programme 'Bargain Hunt'!

The following morning when eventually we were washed and dressed, a discussion started as to what should be done next. Anne had obviously grown quite fond of Eva and to some extent this was a two-way admiration society. It led to Eva putting forward a proposal to the rest of us.

"Anne has been so kind, driving us all the way to the City of London and back that I think we owe her a big thank you and whilst Jon is still around," she smiled in the direction of the window where one assumed that Jon was standing, ". . . we can help her with Jon's funeral and some other things that she would like us to do."

This latter part seemed a bit vague but nevertheless everyone agreed that since we were not in any hurry to go anywhere, we could indeed spend some time with Anne in her 'hour of need'. Had I known what these 'other things' were I might not have been so keen to stay.

In the following few days, the focus of all our attentions was on the funeral and burial of the body of Jon Stow at the London church of St Andrew Undershaft where it was Anne's intention to have a monument built, comprising of a terracotta figure of him in honour of all the important work her husband had done. It was much like a number of funerals I had been to, with one large exception. The person whose body was being buried was stood next to me! Eva in her own 'minxish' way had put her arm on my shoulder half-way through the graveside interment of the coffin in order to show me the smiling face of the man whose body was being lowered into the ground. I really hoped that no-one was watching me because I had to smile at the surreal scene that I was witnessing.

After the funeral, we all, including the deceased, returned to the house in Lime Street, where Anne and Rebecca had done Jon proud with the limited resources available and we had a 17th century banquet almost fit for a king. Anne had invited back to the house a number of her (and Jon's) closest friends, including Ben Jonson a dramatist, poet and actor of some renown. It was a real celebration of what had been a life of achievement of a very special man. At that moment I decided that I wanted Eva at my funeral so I could surprise a few people who might say negative things about my life on this earth. All ghosts should have the recourse to combat negative things said about them at their funerals!

Ben Jonson was a well-built man of about thirty-five with longish, thickset hair and a beard. It seemed unusual that such a young man would become good friends with Jon as their age difference was almost forty years. He was, for the most part, the centre of attention of the assembled mourners. He waxed lyrical about Jon but also about himself and the plays he had written. He had been born a Protestant, his family coming from the Scottish Borders, but had converted to Catholicism some seven years before. This at a difficult time for Catholics in the latter stages of the reign of Elizabeth I. Apparently, according to Mr Jonson, this conversion had happened whilst he was on remand in the jail at Newgate, charged with manslaughter. He had been to Westminster School but had decided not to go to university; instead he 'was put to the trade of bricklaying'. His wife, also called Ann, who stood by his side throughout, looked extremely sad as he recounted how their daughter Mary had died at six months old and their son Benjamin had died of the plague only last year at the age of seven.

It was then that the 'other things' we were there to help Anne with started to happen. There was a sudden banging at the door. Anne went to open the door but before she could, four rather large men burst through it knocking her to the ground. They rushed towards Ben Jonson, who instinctively backed away, knocking over a chair as he did so. There was quite a scuffle as a table was overturned, spilling the food that had been placed on top of it.

As Ben was being man-handled out of the door, one of the men read out a statement from the authorities saying that Mr Jonson had been arrested because the play that he had written called 'Eastward Ho' had anti-Scottish sentiments written in it and on the orders of King James I of England and VI of Scotland, he was to be arrested.

They were struggling down the path with Ben, who was not going quietly, when Eva stepped forward and touched the arm of the man who had just read out Ben's alleged misdemeanour. His action was immediate and must have been baffling to others. He screamed and ran as fast as his long legs would take him down Lime Street. The other three men stopped in amazement at his reaction. They still had hold of Ben who had, like them, stopped struggling when they heard the piercing scream. Eva calmly walked over to the group of four and placed her hands on the two nearest to her. The watching crowd, which was growing by the minute, then witnessed a second unexplained bizarre set of events. The three men looked forward with fixed gazes and then looked at each other and in unison screamed and were soon in pursuit of their colleague down Lime Street. For his part Mr Benjamin Jonson, famous playwright, poet and actor, fainted!

It is difficult to know where to start, but perhaps the most important thing that had happened was that a very elegant 'roofed' carriage with two very obedient horses had been left by the fleeing men and while all around were more concerned with Mr Jonson's well-being, Eva and I took the opportunity to lead the horses and their carriage quietly away around the back of the house to the stable. Provided the men didn't return too soon, the carriage would mean that we would not have to take Anne's carriage to continue our journey. Eva had already spoken to me earlier about not being happy about taking Anne's carriage which would leave her to do a lot of walking or the great expense of buying another.

Once Ben had recovered and was back inside the house, he started, as any actor would, to embellish the story of what had just happened.

"Jon was standing there with a halo around his head, dressed all in white; in heaven smiling at us as if he were not dead!"

You could tell that those listening were not wholly convinced about the vision Ben had described, but at least six and possibly seven of those present were beginning to build up a picture of the truth.

Much later, when all had gone, including the somewhat shaken Mr and Mrs Jonson, the conversation turned to the events of the day.

"Jon has had the best funeral and wake that anyone could have had and he has really enjoyed it, haven't you Jon?" Anne said and, although she could not hear his reply as Eva was not close by, she took a 'yes' answer as being a certainty.

It transpired that Anne had suspected that something might happen at the funeral. Both Jon and Ben had been, for some time, under suspicion from King James' authorities of being Catholic sympathisers. Arrests of such sympathisers had been common since the start of King James' reign in 1603.

Only Eva and I knew that things were going to get a whole lot worse after the 5th November.

The journey to Windsor

I had decided that, while we had the chance, we needed to discuss the problem of dates with Jon and of course Eva. The problem was that it was now the middle of April 1605 and to complete our task of reuniting Valentine with his mother Hester we had to advance somehow to some time after 1642. We could hardly deposit Valentine at Great Staughton Manor before he or his mother were born!

It would be quite traumatic for the youngster, if he ever found out who his mother was, to also find out that he was, in fact, older than she was!

No! We had to find a way of completing the circle so to speak.

Jon was a very intelligent man. He would eventually understand our predicament and might be able to offer a valuable solution.

The opportunity arose when Anne took Rebecca and the children to find suitable clothing for the journey that lay ahead, to replace the tattered clothes they wore. Eva deemed herself to be quite happy with her 'hand-me down' clothes even though they were beginning to smell a little. She must have sensed that a talk with Jon was more important.

Valentine was to be bought new clothes too. Anne was being incredibly generous, or maybe she was just repaying Eva for the extra time that she was having with her husband.

Whilst the rest were out of the house, Eva explained to Jon about our 'time' problem and since I was in contact with her, I could listen in on the questions he put to her.

"You need to move from now to September 1642 just after a battle, you say, the Battle of . . ." he paused.
"Edgehill. It's near Banbury," Eva completed his sentence.
"That is quite a problem and I have no experience in moving forward in time."
"But you might meet someone who can help us."
"How?"
"Well, there are these 'corridors of transit' that you will be able to move down and the way they work is that they allow people who have died to go to special places in their lives, where they were born, where they died and places that meant something special to them when they were alive. John's grandmother had my

bedroom as a special place as sadly that was where she died."

"And where this whole thing started," I pointed out with a bit of a sigh.
"Her name was Eva as well. She was a lovely lady," Eva continued unconcerned about my comment.
"Still is," I reflected.
"Yes, still is," Eva smiled.

"But I have never been to Banbury or Edgehill," Jon brought us back to the problem.
"Yes, well Jon that's why we need someone else to help us. I think that the person needs to have a special place around Warwick because that's near to where we are going. They should be able to visit that place around now, perhaps born in April 1605 and maybe dies near Banbury around 1642. No wait a minute, it needs to be later, about 1645."

Jon said exactly what I was thinking. "That sounds very complicated. I am not sure I will be able to help you."

"Why 1645?" I asked, "We took him in 1642."
"Well time has moved on and Valentine has grown! Hester said that he was about nine months old when we accidently took him with us, and now I guess he is about two and a half years old. So we cannot take him back to 1642. I think that 1645 would make him about three years old."

That was logic I hadn't even thought about!

"That means they die at the age of forty years." Eva continued, "I don't suppose the book mentions a plague about 1645 near Oxford?"
"We seem to be clutching at straws, but I'll have a look."

"I don't know how you will find this person, Jon, but our hopes rest with you." There was a slight hint of desperation in Eva's voice.
"I will see what I can do, but I haven't really understood what powers, if any, I have through being dead."

There are just some statements that you never thought you would hear and for me that was one of them! The one thing that Eva hadn't mentioned was the fact that Jon would eventually disappear from Eva's view once he left Limbo. We really did not know how much time he had to come up with a solution.

That evening I scoured the book for plagues!

Bolton in 1644 and Preston in 1643 were mentioned, neither being the right time or the right place, as many who died in it might have thought. London in 1603 and of course the one in 1665 when, the book said, one sixth of the population of London died of the plague. It mentioned the fact that 666 was the sign of the beast and they really feared that 1666 would bring an even bigger plague. A big beast did arrive only not in the guise of a plague but, of course, a great fire!

———

We said that we would stay with Anne until the end of April hoping that Jon would come up with a person who would allow us to finish our mission and go home. Each day we wondered whether Jon would disappear for good. We had no plan B. Jon really was our only hope. We were not sure where he went or what he did but there were long periods he was not visible even with Eva's powers.

According to 'the book' we needed to be somewhere around Warwick on 6th November, the day after the fateful capture of Guy Fawkes. We had plenty of time to get there with the carriage that we had stolen after the incident with Ben Jonson. The days would get warmer at first and that would be the ideal time to travel, when there was lots of daylight. There was, of course, danger. Anne had warned us of the increasing number of thieves that lined the roads out of London in the direction of Oxford, which would be our starting point in our journey to Holbeche House. One man, one woman and four children in a slow moving carriage would be an ideal opportunity for any would-be thieves.

We made preparation for the journey. Anne gave us yet more in the way of money, food, drink, clothes and directions. Jon had mentioned that King James had given him something in the way of a pension for all the good things that he had done for the City of London. Sadly, he had not had much time whilst alive to enjoy the fruits of his labour and the belated recognition by King James of all his important work.

The only thing I was a little uneasy about, in the nature of the gifts Anne gave us, was the musket. It was a matchlock musket. I had encountered them before but was definitely not proficient in their operation. Someone once had told me how they operated but I had never fired one. You had to go through a very precise routine in order to fire them. Firstly they required a match, hence the name, but not the kind of match with which someone from the 21st century would be familiar. The 'match' was a cord which had been specially made with chemicals in it. Once alight, this cord would glow at the end and it was this, when brought into contact with gunpowder, which ignited the charge in the barrel of the weapon. The bullets which flew out of the barrel were like little marbles. They could, when at speed, smash any bone or human organ that got in their way. The matchlock musket could be lethal but didn't seem to be that accurate apart from at close range, and when it rained hard could be useless, not to mention the accidental explosion of the gunpowder in the pan.

Thus as a gift, with the expectation that I could use it efficiently, it made me nervous.

With little contact with Jon for about three days, I sensed that Eva was a little edgy when we finally set off for Oxford on 2nd May. The 'stolen' coach and horses, which for some reason had not been reclaimed, were as ideal as anything we could have acquired in the 17th century, although a car with a full tank of petrol would have been better.

The children, with the exception of Valentine, had had a great deliberation on what to call the two horses. I suspected that Eva had started the discussion as she had always been one to name living things. On our last journey through the seventeenth century we had had two horses, the first had been named Dodger as in the 'Artful Dodger' of 'Oliver' fame because I had stolen it! The second was called 'Cropredy' because that was the village where we bought the horse. Finally, there was a stag called Purkiss. For the life of me I cannot remember why Eva called a large deer that but it had been a great-life saver and a wonderful friend to her. The current discussion ended with the names 'Bits' and 'Bobs', although I was not too sure which horse was which.

Rebecca said that she could take the reins as it was something she had done when she was younger and maybe sensed my reluctance to do so. The carriage didn't have the automatic gears I was used to!

This left Eva, Charlotte and Jacob to look after Valentine in the carriage which made them all feel very important.

It was a very sad departure for all concerned. We had all grown fond of Anne and her great hospitality had been much appreciated, but we had to move on at some time and now seemed the best time. Yet again, she warned us to be careful and to keep the musket handy at all times.

Anne had given us the 'map', for want of a better word, that Jon had been an instigator in producing about seven years ago. There were few signs but there again there weren't the hundreds of roads leading out of London. The thought of taking our coach and horses on the M25 and then up the M40 to Oxford brought a smile to my face.

Oxford, according to Anne, was about fifty to sixty miles away. We could have probably done that in a day's travelling, but Rebecca thought that we should take it a little more leisurely for Valentine's sake. I have said before that Valentine was one of the most placid of children I had ever come across and apart from the usual discomfitures which I won't describe in detail, he seemed to take everything in his stride. He seemed to have been passed from 'pillar to post' as the saying goes, but for most of the time he grinned and chortled, mostly at Eva's antics and I didn't want to know what they entailed.

The road out of London was to take us over the Chiltern Hills. Jon's map indicated that we needed to cross the River Thames at Staines on our way to what we thought might be our overnight stay at the town of Windsor. Staines was about fifteen miles away and Windsor a further five miles. Part of the journey seemed to take us on what Jon had indicated as 'Drover Roads'. Anne had tried to explain that these roads were very wide, used by drovers who brought cattle and other livestock to the markets of London. It must have been quite a task driving a hundred or so sheep and cows for fifty to a hundred miles to market. The pitfalls were obvious and didn't confine themselves just to a cow getting lost 'en route'. The stealing of livestock must have been widespread.

As we rode steadily out of the outer areas of London in the warm May sunshine, I couldn't help but think of all those 'cowboy' films I had watched as a youngster. Not just because I was riding in a coach, but because of all the films I had seen where cattle were herded along the wide plains of America by young men on horse back with their gun-belts and rifles. Sadly I found myself humming 'Oh! The Deadwood Stage is a-heading on over the hills . . . .'! I could safely say that nobody else in the carriage would recognise the song and it wasn't just because of my poor humming!

With frequent stops and some slight holdups for cattle we arrived in the town of Staines in the middle of the afternoon. The town seemed to consist of one very wide street suitable and no doubt used for a market. It had a number of pleasant-looking houses and a couple of places that looked like staging posts for coaches such as ours. We stopped in order to let the horses rest and drink some well-deserved water. A man approached the coach and asked if we wanted to exchange horses. Before I could answer, Rebecca took charge and said that as we had not travelled far the horses were fine.

"I have heard stories of what they do," she said, "they take our good horses and exchange them for old nags and charge you money."

"Sounds like the 17th century version of a used-car salesman," I said without thinking.

"You'd better explain to Rebecca what a 'used-car salesman' is John," commented Eva since she had noticed the frown on Rebecca's face.

"Maybe some other time."

"I'd like to know now," said Rebecca with a smile on her face only matched by the one on Eva's.

"Well, we have a different kind of coach in the 21st century and it is called a car, and when you want to sell your car to buy a new one you can exchange it with the help of a 'used-car salesman'."

"Four out of ten," said Eva in a mock teacher-type of voice.

"How does a car work? Does it have horses to pull it along?"

This wasn't the time to try and explain 'horse-power', even if I could.

"No. Someone invents something called an 'engine' which pulls the car along."

This wasn't going well but I sensed that with Eva's help Rebecca was getting me to 'dig holes' from which there might be no escape.

"I'll explain a little more later." Both Eva and Rebecca smiled. I was beginning to like Rebecca. She was confident, intelligent and possessed quite a sense of humour. She, like everybody else, had taken to Eva and since she had just lost one daughter, I suspect that, if you ever can replace a daughter of your own, she had a ready-made substitute in Eva.

Rebecca went to buy some food and drink with some of the money Anne had given us. She was obviously the best person for such an errand.

After about half an hour we were on the road again across the River Thames and on towards Windsor. It was hard to believe that just a few miles from here in about four hundred years' time, great metal planes carrying hundreds of people would be taking off for destinations thousands of miles away. I didn't fancy explaining that to Rebecca. She would have laughed and said that it was impossible for heavy things to fly through the air. Furthermore explaining it to others might well have got you burned to death as a witch. How time changes things! Would people from the year 2400 think the same of us in 2008? How primitive our travel methods are? What other inventions would four hundred years bring?

My explanation of 'cars' did not take place, as within an hour and a half we were in the town of Windsor. I expected it to be really 'posh' but there was clearly a lot of poverty in Windsor. The streets were badly-made and the houses were much poorer than the ones we had seen in Staines.

The problem now was to find somewhere to rest for the night. You can never find a Travel Lodge when you need one!

Rebecca suggested that we could rest down by the River Thames in view of Windsor Castle, one of the residences of King James. Although the castle was clearly of motte and bailey construction, you could just make out some tennis courts which were probably the work of Henry VIII, who had constructed some at the Palace at Hampton Court. It was clear why that location had been used to build a castle. It must have had commanding views over the River Thames. The castle seemed to be surrounded by parklands and it was here that Rebecca had decided to 'camp' for the night.

"We don't need permission to be here?" I asked her as she finally brought the coach to rest by the bank of the river.

"No," she said firmly, "this land belongs to us all."

The not-so-dreaming spires of Oxford

Eva hadn't said much about what she might have seen on the journey to Windsor. I assumed that if there was anything of note, she would have mentioned it. It was clear that Jon was not around and in a way our hopes of successfully completing our mission seemed to have disappeared with him. I tried to broach the subject casually the next morning.

"I suppose there's been no sign of Jon or anybody else who might be able to help us."
"No, not really. I was worried when we were in Staines though. Did you notice that group of men at the place we stopped?"
"No, I was busy trying to explain what a car was, if you remember!"
"Well, they were looking at us in a strange way and I think that they were talking about us."

"Oh well, they're gone now."

"That's the point. They're over there, at the other side of that large tree. They have obviously been following us."

"Maybe they're just going in the same direction to Oxford."

"Could be, but something in me senses that we're in danger."

I never argued with Eva's feelings. They were well-honed and dead accurate.

"What do you suggest?"

"Difficult really. We are sitting ducks so to speak, even with you and that very untrustworthy musket. There were three of them but I can only see two at the moment. I assume that they will all have guns of some description. If they decide to do something, the odds are not good for us."

"But we haven't got much for them to steal."

"They don't know that. With this coach we probably look like quite a rich family, mother and father and four children. We are an easy target for robbery."

"They wouldn't do it here though?"

"No, that's true but there may be woods or hills coming up and they probably know the best place for a robbery."

"Aren't you being a bit pessimistic?"

"Remember what Anne said about loads of thieves being on the outskirts of London where travellers unaware of the dangers are being robbed on a daily basis."

"OK, we have to think of a plan to keep us safe. I suppose we could just walk over there and tell them that we have nothing worth stealing."

"Perhaps there's a better plan A, John. How much further to Oxford?"
"About forty miles. It should take us about ten or eleven hours."
"Will we need new horses?"
"No, I wouldn't think so. We are not pushing them and we are giving them plenty of rests."
"How fast do you think they can pull this coach?"
"On these roads with six people? Not fast. We couldn't outrun three horsemen if that was what you were thinking."
"We could do with Purkiss!"

As I have mentioned before, Purkiss was a magnificent stag, who on our last mission had saved our lives whilst we were on the run from similar horsemen. Sadly he gave up his own life in doing so.

"Let me talk to Rebecca. Maybe she knows a bit more about the road we are travelling on."

Sadly, Rebecca had never been to Oxford in her life. She said that she had been to Windsor on a number of occasions with her father when she was young, but not to the city that housed England's first University and the one that Charles I was to make the capital of England for a short time during the Civil War.

We set off after an hour or so in the direction of the Chiltern Hills which lay between Windsor and Oxford. With no wing mirrors, I glanced over my shoulder several times to try and catch sight of the three horsemen. They were nowhere to be seen. If they were going to attempt to rob us then they would not have much trouble catching us up and since, according to Eva, one of them might have gone on ahead, the only question was where the best place to attack might be.

I know it may seem strange but I had every confidence in the fact that Eva would come up with a good plan A. She was no ordinary thirteen-year-old and had had the imagination and powers to come up with some strange solutions to our problems. I had seen her work at first hand on a number of occasions. My main worry was for the children. Musket fire, if it came to that, was not that accurate from any distance except really close-up and a stray bullet could do some real damage to a child.

The weather was still good although there looked to be a number of rain clouds on the horizon. 'Sunny with occasional showers' would be my forecast.

Jacob and Charlotte seemed excited, as they might be with a big adventure ahead. They were in the coach with Rebecca looking after Valentine and Eva was up front with me.

"Any sign of them?" I asked.

"No. They seem to have disappeared."

"OK. Oxford, the City of Dreaming Spires, here we come."

———

The wide Drover Road took us to the foot of the hills and we pulled Bits and Bobs over to the side of the road for a well-earned rest. There was a small stream close by that I thought would be a useful watering-hole for them.

The children tumbled out of the carriage and started to play a game of 'tig'. Although Jacob was a year or two younger than Eva and Charlotte he had no problem dodging and out-running the two girls. They temporarily disappeared behind rocks and trees. Rebecca and I were not overly worried about this disappearance as there appeared to be no one around, and Rebecca had her arms full with attempting to feed Valentine.

Suddenly there were shouts and screams and the two girls came running into sight.

"They've got Jacob!" they screamed in unison. "They've got Jacob!"

"Who have?" Rebecca shouted, but before they could answer, we could see exactly who had Jacob.

Before us stood the three men whom Eva had seen in Staines and again in Windsor. The one on the right had a firm grip on a struggling Jacob. The other two had their pistols drawn and pointed in our direction. All three wore masks.

"What do you want?" It seemed the only sensible question.

Naturally, Rebecca was a little more distressed and ran forward towards the man holding Jacob. She was felled by a blow to the head from the man in the middle and seemed to be unconscious.

"We want all your money and the gold and jewellery that you have," said the slightly taller man in the middle. "Everything of value!"

"We have nothing. We are poor travellers."

"With a coach and horses like that!"

Whilst Charlotte had run to comfort her mother who seemed to be stirring a little, Eva spoke in a very calm voice given what she had just witnessed.

"We do have money. Lots of money but it is in our house in Oxford. I am the daughter of Sir Thomas Tresham and he will pay you handsomely for the release of Jacob, his son."

The men looked at each other as if to say 'do we believe this girl?' I had not got a clue where Eva had picked up the information on Sir Thomas Tresham. His son Francis had been to Thomas Percy's house in Westminster a couple of times but we had hardly spoken to him.

"You can search the carriage but you will find no gold or money but I can assure you my father will pay for the release of his son."

The centre man nodded to his accomplice who walked passed us and jumped up into the carriage. After a few minutes and with finding nothing but a sleeping child, he returned to confirm Eva's story.

"Nothing but rags and food, and this old musket!"

"We never travel with money or gold. It's too dangerous. We are on our way back from London to our home in Oxford." Eva pressed the point yet again.

"Fetch the horses, Frank. The rest of you on the carriage." he said waving his pistol in the general direction of it."

"What about the lady you hit? The person my father has chosen to look after his children."

"Get her on the carriage!" He showed little compassion for what he had done.

Frank brought three horses into view and with that the third member of the group released Jacob who immediately ran to the aid of his mother who had regained her feet. She had a large swelling on her left temple and the blow had clearly broken the skin as blood could be seen on her cheek.

"I don't suppose we have any Germolene?" I whispered to Eva. She smiled and nodded.

By this time the men had removed their masks. I never really understood the wearing of masks. The eyes are the most recognisable feature of a face and I would recognise these three pairs of eyes until my dying day. I felt very angry but Eva had defused the situation and bought us time in which to put a plan together.

The, as yet, unnamed man who had held Jacob so firmly was the stockiest of the three and he was designated to ride at the front with me. The children and the injured Rebecca, who was probably getting her first dose of antiseptic cream, were in the back. I had had the foresight to bring some Germolene on the first trip and it appeared that in many ways Eva had packed her haversack with many of the same items as I had.

So there we were; the six of us riding in a carriage being escorted and chaperoned by two armed men on horseback together with a spare horse and a 'taxi' driver.

I felt quite reassured that no one else would attempt an ambush but you never quite knew what might happen. Punch, yes that was the name of our 'taxi' driver, was quite an affable man. Although he looked the strongest of the three, he had quite a pleasant face, a bit like David Stockdale in that 60s series 'Heartbeat'. He had sort of a vacant look and there were times in our conversations when clearly he did not understand what I had said. It could, of course, have been the way I spoke but there was a suggestion of limited intelligence about his demeanour. It was clear who the ring leader was in this 'gang'. The 'middle man', whose name had as yet not been mentioned, kept barking out orders to Punch as if he was some sort of 'back seat driver'. It clearly irritated Punch who often cursed under his breath but said nothing out loud.

Oxford was still a good way off, but we negotiated what must have been the Chiltern Hills without too much of a problem and Bits and Bobs still looked strong.

"We'll stop at the top of this hill, Punch. Pull over on that grass so the horses can feed," came the command.

It had started to rain so our final resting place was modified so as to be under a group of oak trees for shelter.

Punch brought Bits and Bobs to a halt and jumped down. He showed the compassion that his leader lacked and went to help a still slightly groggy Rebecca down from the carriage. The aroma of Germolene was a welcome familiar smell. Eva had, as expected, done a good job as nurse.

"Are you feeling better?" I asked Rebecca.

"Yes I am fine. That, what did Eva call it, er . . . ointment was most soothing."

And as an afterthought whispered, "Is it from the future?"

"Yes it is an antiseptic. It will make sure no infection will get into the wound. Is your eyesight good?"

She gave me a strange look. "I mean you don't have blurred vision, do you?"

Another strange look came my way.

"You can see alright?"

"Why yes."

"Sometimes a blow to the head can affect how you can see."

"No, I am fine but have a slight headache. Do you have any magic potion for headaches?"

"Have you any Paracetamol?" I asked Eva as she was in the process of getting out of the carriage with Valentine in her arms.

"Who do you think I am, NHS direct?"

I looked at Rebecca and smiled. "I'll leave that explanation until later!"

We rested for about half an hour. The three men chatted to each other, no doubt planning what they would do when they got to Oxford. It was difficult to see what their options were, but their greed for money was driving them on.

I managed to have a brief word with Eva. "What is your plan when we get to Oxford?"

"I don't know. I just tried to put them off with that story."

"Where did you get the name Sir Thomas Tresham from?"

"I overheard it when his son Francis came one day to the house in Westminster. Apparently his father has lots of money and was building some kind of religious monument near er . . . Peterborough, I think. They were building it as a monument to the Catholics but were trying to build it so that Protestants like Queen Elizabeth didn't recognise it was one."

"Anyway well done! I think I can help with the question 'where do you live?'"

"I hadn't thought of that. I was just going to blag my way around until I thought of something."

"Well, I think that in Oxford there is a Banbury Road. I've stayed there a couple of times. Banbury Road was the street that my daughter Jayne walked down in her first pair of high heels. I say 'walked' but she was clinging on to me for most of the way. Quite amusing really."

"My dad says I can't have high heels until I am sixteen."

"Jayne must have been about that age. Anyway remember you live on Banbury Road. You haven't said who I am as yet."

"You can be one of the servants or do they have chauffeurs in the 17th century?"

"OK, that sounds reasonable. Don't say too much though. They might rumble that your story isn't true and then we are in trouble."

"I don't suppose that Jon is around or anyone that might help us?"

Eva smiled.

"He is! I am not saying anything just yet until we are in a position to act. The less you know the better." That put me in my place.

"OK, you have come up with some good solutions in the past so I have to trust you now."

She smiled again.

On orders from the 'man in the middle' we all ascended the carriage and resumed our previous places. Punch was still a bit talkative so I decided to ask him a few questions.

"You know Sir Thomas is very rich. How much do you think the child is worth?"

"Dick thinks we might get as much as a thousand pounds."

"Wow! That is a lot of money."

"It would mean I don't need to do all this robbing. I hate doing this to folk, but I needs the money for my family."

"You have children?"

"Yes two. Two boys."

"What are you going to do when you get to Oxford?"

He glanced at me as if to say, 'what's it got to do with you?'

"Not sure. Dick says we will threaten to kill the children if he doesn't pay up."
"Kill all four children! Could you really do that Punch?"

He hesitated and then started to answer but thought better of it. Presumably, Dick had quite a hold over him and he would do whatever Dick wanted.

As we entered the outskirts of Oxford, from what I imagine was the South-East, Dick called out for Punch to stop the coach on what seemed some sort of parkland in order to let the horses rest and graze. His ulterior motive seemed to be to have a chance to talk tactics with the other two as he summoned Punch down from his driving seat. There was just a moment when I could have grabbed the reins of the horses and made off, but I noticed that both Charlotte and Eva had got out of the coach as well. I probably wouldn't have got far but could have made quite a scene with the men and their guns. But with Eva and Charlotte left behind, it would only have made matters worse. I resolved that I would leave the planning to Eva.

I jumped down and went to see how Rebecca was. She still had quite a bit of swelling and the colour of her skin was turning from red to purple as the bruising 'came out'.

"I am fine," came her answer to my question, "Eva gave me something called a tablet."
"What?"

"She did tell me the name of it but . . ."

"It was an aspirin tablet. It's all my mother had left in the bathroom cabinet!" came a voice from behind, "Anyway it worked even if it wasn't what you said."

She sounded hurt, as if she had got it wrong.

"Hey, I am not complaining and neither is Rebecca."

"No, I feel fine, Eva."

"Has Dick said anything to you?"

"Who?"

"Dick is the name of the bossy ringleader."

"No, not yet. They are talking over there. Seems quite heated, as if the're having an argument."

"It's difficult to know what they are going to do. Wait a minute, Dick's coming over!"

"You girl!" He shouted at Eva. "I have some questions for you!"

"Of course. You want to know where I live."

Although this seemed the obvious question, it seemed to take the wind out of his sails a little. Maybe it was the confident way Eva addressed him.

"We want your servant here to go to your father's house and tell him that we want one thousand pounds delivered straight away to the New Inn."

"Where is that exactly?" Eva responded.

"Don't you know?"

"No I don't. I don't frequent ale houses!"

He ignored Eva's comment. "It's near Carfax Tower by St Martin's Church, just off Cornmarket Street," he retorted in an aggressive manner.

"I know where that is, sir," I lied.

"Good. I want you to bring the money there tomorrow at noon. Then I will tell you where Sir Thomas can find his children unharmed."

"Won't it take him a long time to get so much money?"

"He's a rich man. If he wants to, he will be able to find it quickly otherwise he will never see his children alive again."

Rebecca gasped. It had only just dawned on her that her children, Charlotte and Jacob, were also being targeted as Sir Thomas' off-spring. I half-expected her to deny the fact that they belonged to Sir Thomas, which would have placed Eva's story in some jeopardy and all of us in some danger. To her credit she said nothing but had gone quite pale at the thought of what might happen.

"Where is the house?"

"It's on Banbury Road," I replied saving Eva the bother of remembering the name of the road I had said.

"You can walk from here."

"Can I have a word with Mistress Eva?" I said, as politely as I could.

"You can say whatever you want in front of me now and then go." Dick was not in the mood for us having a conversation that did not involve him.

"Tell Mr. Stow that he has to hang around as long as possible and make as much mischief as he can."

All three people in front of me had what can only be described as blank faces. Eventually, Eva said, "If I see him I will tell him."

Dick must have thought we had gone potty and simply turned to me and said, "On your way and remember what I said. No money and the children and this serving wench all die."

———

I walked on into Oxford with my stomach churning over and those butterflies that you get when you are in some form of shock. What was I going to do? I had no special powers, no money and no knowledge of where Banbury Road was. Not that that mattered. There was nobody at any house on that street that could help. Sir Thomas Tresham was not a fictitious character; he existed, but nowhere near Oxford.

I was really surprised to find that Oxford was a walled city. It certainly wasn't when I made my first visit to it in 1976, or was this the first time I had been in Oxford?

Nobody stopped me as with many others I walked through what I assume was the most southern gate. I wandered aimlessly for an hour, along Blue Boar Street and Bear Street. Why are streets given such ridiculous names? If they saw a bear or a blue boar in Oxford they must be on some form of hallucinogenic medication or be a student! I was thinking of wild plans that are too stupid to recall. Suddenly I saw a slightly familiar building. It was the famous library in Oxford. I knew it as the Bodleian Library. OK, so it wasn't quite the building I had seen in 1976, but the shape of the building and its doors had a familiarity to them.

I looked for the main entrance and entered. I could see what I imagined were students, not quite dressed the way they were in my day.

I could see a man staring at me, perhaps I wasn't quite dressed in the way a man who frequents libraries might be dressed. He was well-groomed with a moustache and a small beard, which seemed to be the style of the time. He approached me and in a very formal way asked if he could help me.

'In for a penny in for a pound' as the saying goes. The only thing I had in my armoury, for what it was worth, was 'information'. However smart this guy was, I was confident that I knew more than he did! Sounds arrogant, but it was all I had. Plan A was to win him over and get him to help me, perhaps lend me one thousand pounds. But somehow, I doubted it!

"I am a self-taught mathematician and I was wondering if I could look at the books you have on calculus."

"Of course, we have several. May I introduce myself? I am Thomas Bodley." he said proudly. Yet another Thomas but not the one I wanted.

"Are you the very person this library is named after?"
He smiled. One brownie point won!
"Yes I am. Do I know you? Are you an academic?"
"No, just someone who is curious about mathematics."

We chatted for some time. I think initially he was testing me on my knowledge of mathematics but clearly he wasn't a mathematician. Apparently, he had been a lecturer in Ancient Greek at Merton College in Oxford, but had become the driving force behind improving an old library; he called it Duke Humfrey's library. It had been in existence for many years but, for reasons he did not go into, it had had hardly any books in it. He had put a lot of his own books into the new improved library; sought donations from other academics and from other countries such as China; and so two years ago the library reopened. It was now a thriving library used by the students and other academics. With a great deal of pride, he told me that they had decided to call it after him, Bodley's Library and with a final flourish he told me that he had been the gentleman usher (whatever that was) to Queen Elizabeth and a year or so ago had been knighted by King James.

This conversation was getting me nowhere and I was feeling very anxious that time was not on my side.

"Do you know Sir Thomas Tresham?" I plunged in without really knowing what I was doing. The better question was 'do you know a rich man who will give me one thousand pounds?' But that seemed a little too abrupt.

"He is a well-known Catholic but he doesn't live in Oxford, somewhere further east I think. Why do you ask?"

"Well, I desperately need help. I am a servant of Sir Thomas," perpetuating the story seemed the best option. "I was escorting some of his children from London to Warwick when we were set upon by thieves. We had no money with us so they are holding the children hostage whilst I find Sir Thomas and obtain from him the one thousand pounds that they are asking for their release."

He looked at me in a strange way.
"Sir, you use words I do not understand and I pride myself that I have a good knowledge of the English language but you talk in such a strange way. Pray what is a 'hostage'?"

"I do apologise. You are right I am not from this area. What I meant to say was that thieves have captured Sir Thomas' children and are threatening to kill them unless I bring one thousand pounds to the New Inn tomorrow at noon."

"That is indeed a problem but I see no way I can help you in the matter." I am not sure that he believed my story.

"Could you at least tell me where the New Inn is located?"

"Yes certainly. It is not far from here."

He gave me some directions but I wasn't really listening. I more or less knew the answer but my mind was on what I should do next. Suddenly Sir Thomas Bodley said; "I do know someone who might be able to help. We have a prison here in Oxford. It's called Bocardo Prison and it's not too far from here."

"How might that help?"

"They may have the names of all the thief-takers in the area."

"Thief-takers? What are they?"

"A thief-taker is a private individual who can be hired to capture criminals," he said in a resigned way as if everybody should know what they were.

I suppose prior to the Police Force coming into being they were like the bounty hunters of the Wild West except they were hired and paid for by the criminals' victims rather than the community or government they served.

"But be very careful, some of the thief-takers are just as corrupt as the criminals they are trying to bring to justice," and with that he turned and walked away.

It seemed a very long shot but the best I had. I had no money and only the vague promise of payment to a thief-taker once the children were released. As I returned to the streets of Oxford, I wondered how Eva was doing; had she hatched a plan to escape?

Somewhere in the distance the chimes of a church bell signalled that it was five o'clock. Would the prison welcome non-custodial guests at this time?

In fact the bells came from St Martin's Church which had a very large tower reaching up some eighty feet. I had decided that the time was not right to visit the prison but to find somewhere safe to rest for the night. A church seemed the right place. I was hungry. We had hidden what was left of Anne Stow's money in a delicate place in Rebecca's clothing where we hoped no one but Rebecca would search! What I needed was an orchard of some type, although in May the fruit would be pretty sour but better than nothing. The other option was begging!

Some strange ideas went through my head. Maybe I could sing for my supper. A bit of busking might get me some food or money or then again it might get me killed. Anyway, all the songs I knew had not been written yet, not for about four hundred years.

The rain had cleared and it was turning into a fine evening, if you had nothing important on your mind that is! Then I saw something I had never seen before, a castle in Oxford. Maybe it was still there in 1976 but I cannot recall seeing it.

I walked around what might have been the south side of the castle to where there seemed to be fields and trees, and maybe the place an orchard might be situated. I crossed a field and then a road that was lined with large trees. In the distance across some parkland, I could see some form of construction with a large tower. From where I stood it looked like a manor house or a religious building.

As I neared the building I could see that, although it had probably seen better days and once upon a time had been a magnificent place for people to live, it was now in ruins and had not been cared for, for some time.

I could see men carrying things out of the building and it looked as if it had become something of a construction site. Clearly one man was in charge, directing what was to be placed where on a waiting horse and cart. The man was elderly and dressed in a form of cassock which marked him out as a man of religion.

I stopped some distance away and observed the proceedings. When the cart was fully laden two of the men departed with it together with the horse that had been patiently waiting and grazing. I took this opportunity to approach the 'man of religion'. As I got closer, I could see that he was indeed quite elderly. I would have put him close to seventy years old. He had a long white beard and a stooped appearance that sadly comes with age.

"Could you help me please, I am looking for food and a place to stay tonight?" Honesty was the best policy.

He studied my somewhat scruffy appearance for a moment and said "You could stay in the old Abbey tonight. It is quite safe now that nearly everything has been taken from it."

"Where are you taking all the things from the Abbey?"

"To Christ Church. The old Abbey hasn't been used for nearly sixty years. Lots of things have been taken to the other churches in Oxford but the Abbey has been looted of nearly everything over the years. They have even taken Great Tom, the bell that used to hang in that tower over there. Many people described that bell as the loudest thing in Oxford, and now it is hanging in Tom Tower at Christ Church. Nearly all of the monastic property has been transferred to Christ Church." He sighed a really heavy sigh as if it was all his fault and he could now do nothing about it.

"Are you the Bishop of Oxford?" I guessed that his age would make him quite high in the hierarchy of religious men.

"Yes, I am Bishop John Bridges. I have been Bishop of Oxford for a year now. King James made me Bishop of Oxford when he came to the throne. Before that, sadly, there had been no bishops in Oxford for about ten years."

He seemed very content telling a complete stranger part of his life story.

"I was the Bishop of Salisbury for nearly thirty years but there has been so much conflict within the Church since King Henry decided on the dissolution of all the abbeys and monasteries."

He seemed genuinely sad about the state of his beloved church.

"Food!" he said as if he had just remembered what I had said. "I have some in the Abbey."

I thought I had better start correctly. "As you can probably tell Bishop, I am not from around here, so what is this old Abbey called?"

"It is or was Osney Abbey which then became Osney Cathedral for a short time. A place for Augustinian monks to live once upon a time. The Abbey, so it is said, dates back to the twelfth century. It is so sad to see it in this sorry state. What did you say your name was?"
"I am also called John."
"Well, John, let's go and eat!"

I felt really comfortable in his presence. He didn't seem concerned about where I had sprung from but clearly sad about his new post and the duty of stripping the Abbey which had stood for five hundred years.

As we entered the building he said. "This Abbey is haunted by magpies!"

I wasn't a great lover of 'thieving' magpies at the best of times when they were alive, so being haunted by dead ones didn't fill me with much joy. The Bishop told me the story of Edith Forne, wife of Robert D'Oyly, the Norman governor of Oxford, who had had the house built originally. Our dear old Edith wasn't perfect and had become one of the mistresses of Henry I, but in order to atone for her sins she persuaded her husband to build a place of religious significance by telling him a story of a dream she had had about chattering magpies. This had been interpreted by a friar as souls in purgatory who needed a church in which to rest. So poor Richard had to build a church!

The Bishop said that Edith was buried in Osney Abbey and showed me the tomb which I could just make out in the failing light. It was at the side of the altar and according to the Bishop; Edith was buried in religious clothes. By the side of the tomb was painted the legendary dream of chattering magpies. I was not too sure I was going to get a good night's sleep on many counts.

I decided to tell him about my predicament and the advice that Sir Thomas Bodley had given me about 'thief-takers'. He wasn't too sure that the Bocardo Prison was the right place to go and said that in the morning he would come back with a man he thought could help.

After we shared the food that he had, he said good bye and started his walk back to his house in Oxford before the light faded completely and I settled down for a quiet night with the magpies!

———

Bishop John Bridges arrived quite early the next morning as promised. I had had a sleepless night thinking about Eva and the magpies, but was sure that I had at least snatched a couple of hours on the Abbey floor.

He introduced me to a 'thief-taker' called Hugh Howson. He was about forty, slim with a well-groomed moustache and for a 'thief-taker' quite a pleasant smile.
I related the story of the kidnap and the three men involved. He thought that he had heard of the gang from others in his trade, but thought that they were more London-based than Oxford. We had around four hours to come up with a plan.

The problem was that the gang was unlikely to all turn up at the New Inn with all their captives. Clearly one of them would be at the rendezvous hoping to collect the one thousand pound ransom but the other two would still be guarding their captives.

Hugh suggested that we go to the New Inn about one hour ahead of schedule, so at about eleven o'clock. He had several fellow 'thief takers' on hand to help out in the situation. The question was how would the member of the gang at the New Inn relay the information back to the other two to say he had got the money and to release the hostages?

The other slight problem was that we did not have one thousand pounds to give him!

Eventually we had a plan but as yet Hugh had not mentioned how much I would owe him for his services.

The plan was simple enough and needed something to pretend to be the money in some form of bag and as the hand over took place, the gang member would be over-powered and not able to get a signal out to any other gang member. A degree of torture would do the rest. Provided one of the other gang-members was not in the pub as well, this would work. It was up to me to search around the pub to find out how many gang members were present and where they were sat. It might be necessary to apprehend more than one of them at the same time.

The only problem with the plan was the timing. If it took too long to get the location of the children and Rebecca out of the gang-member by torture, whoever was guarding them might get suspicious and anything could happen. With the location of the hostages and the men that Hugh could provide, the rest seemed straight forward.

At approximately 10.30am the six men plus the Bishop and I were assembled at the Abbey and ready to start our journey to the New Inn. All but the Bishop and I were armed with some form of firearm.

Eva's story

What I am about to relate now is, for me, a bit of an anti-climax, because when the eight of us arrived at the New Inn ready to do battle with criminal elements of the 17th century, all we found was Rebecca and four smiling children. They were, I think, pleased to see me but were curious as to why I had such a bodyguard including an elderly clergyman.

Sulkily, I told Eva and the rest how resourceful I had been in recruiting men to deal with the situation. In truth I was recounting the luck I had had in meeting Bishop Bridges. I felt cheated that my or our plan had not been put into operation. I had, of course, to apologize to Hugh and his not-so-merry men that I no longer needed them. Rebecca realized my embarrassment and offered to buy them all a beer at the New Inn. That went some way towards placating the men.

"We ought to get back to the coach before anyone decides to steal it," said Rebecca. "John will really want to know what has happened, won't you John?"

I had to smile. As ever, I had underestimated the powers that Eva had because I was sure that she was at the bottom of this 'great escape'.

We returned the mile or so journey by foot to where the coach had apparently remained since I had left it the day before. I carried Valentine, who in his good-natured way chuckled whenever I pulled silly faces at him. Why do semi-intelligent adults go 'ga ga' when faced with a young child?

As we sat there in front of the coach on what was turning out to be a very hot May afternoon, Eva began the story that everyone but me had seen at first hand.

"Just after you had gone, Rebecca and I were talking about what we might do. We agreed that apart from Dick, the other two didn't seem the sort to kill children. They appeared to be family men who had fallen on hard times. Dick, however, was different and had a mean streak as he showed when he hit Rebecca. We both felt that he was the man we had to target. Get him out of the way and the other two wouldn't have the heart to put up much of a fight."

"You talk as if you and Rebecca were two prize fighters that could take on people in a fight!"

"Just listen. There's more to beating someone than beating them up," she snapped. "That didn't come out quite right, but you know what I mean. Anyway we had a piece of luck. Dick sent the other two into Oxford on some errand this morning, probably to check the New Inn over for the exchange. I was feeding Valentine some manchet when it happened."

"What happened?"

"This!" She touched me lightly on the arm and pointed to a smiling Jon Stow!

"Hi Jon. Nice to see you again." Probably not the usual thing that you might say to someone who has been dead for a month or so!

"Eva is a remarkable young woman. You should be very proud of her!"

"Oh I am," I said without any idea of just how remarkable she had been this time.

"She took on that ruffian single handed."

"That's not true Jon. I couldn't have done it without you and Rebecca."

"And me!" piped in Jacob, yet again.

"And me!" said Charlotte, not to be outdone by her little brother.

"OK just what did the five of you do? I am beginning to feel a little sorry for Dick."

"Do you remember the way we scared off those Cavaliers who threatened Frank, Agnes and little Alice?"

"Vaguely." On our last visit we had encountered some obnoxious men who had tried to forcibly convert the family, who had kindly let us stay with them, from normal law-abiding citizens to soldiers who would fight for King Charles. I remembered that Eva's tactic had involved some gruesome-looking dead people!

"Well I got Charlotte and Jacob to introduce Dick to a couple of Jon's friends, Peter and Paula!"

I really wasn't looking forward to meeting Eva's newly made friends but knew that it was inevitable. My first viewing of Henry Pickering, who had died a most violent death, was one I would remember for the rest of my life, but nothing and I repeat nothing could have prepared me for my first sight of Peter and Paula!

I have never been good at accurately describing people and probably wouldn't be too good at picking out potential villains in a police line-up, but trust me I would have recognized these two anywhere. Where do I begin?

OK, the most obvious feature was that they were headless! Apparently, I learned later from Jon, they had been recently beheaded near North Gate after being imprisoned in Bocardo Prison for running a house of ill-repute.

I only need to add that their clothes were drenched in blood. I was about to ask the obvious when, as if by magic, their heads appeared exactly where one would expect them to be positioned.

"It's a trick that only they know how to do," said Eva as she observed my utter amazement. "Jon met them in Limbo and they agreed to help us out. They were brilliant."

"OK, so what happened? I dread to think."

"Simple really. Charlotte, Jacob and I pretended to play 'ring a ring o' roses'. I taught them it beforehand when we were playing. When the time was right, Jacob reached out for Dick to join in. He was a bit reluctant to start with, but eventually he held Jacob's hand. Jacob held Charlotte's hand and she held mine and in that way we introduced him to the gruesome twosome of Peter and Paula."

"OK he was shocked and slightly stunned maybe by the sight of them but once he dropped Jacob's hand in shock, his horrible vision would disappear," I suggested.

"Ah well, that's when Rebecca took her revenge with that bloodied piece of wood over there. It was all in the timing."

"I must say that I really enjoyed it," Rebecca interjected, "although I do still have some splinters of wood in my hands. Eva has used some of that ointment and removed most of the splinters. They feel better now."

"He really shouldn't go around hitting women," said Eva.

Everyone agreed and nodded. Although Eva had dropped the contact with me, I had a vision of Peter and Paula nodding in a very precarious manner.

"So what happened when Frank and Punch arrived back?"

"We thought that it would be a bit unfair to treat them in the same violent way, since they had not been as aggressive as Dick."

"But I assume they had a visitation from the spirit world as Dick had had?"

"Sort of," replied Eva.

Rebecca smiled, either at the use of Eva's English language or in the knowledge of the tale to come."

"OK. What 'sort of'?"

"Well we had tied Dick up and the four of us dragged him behind those trees over there and Rebecca acted as a sentry over him with her piece of wood. Charlotte, Jacob and I acted all innocent when the men arrived and said we had no idea where Dick had gone. I could see that they thought that it was strange that Dick would leave us all alone when we could easily escape. Suddenly Punch said that maybe he had gone to relieve himself but it was clear that Frank wasn't too happy with the situation and he started to look around the carriage. We had agreed that Frank was going to be the more difficult of the two remaining men as Punch was a bit of a sweetie!"

"I take it that 'a bit of a sweetie' are your words and not what Rebecca would have said?"

Rebecca smiled, "Eva explained what that meant earlier and I agreed."

Somehow I doubted that. Rebecca did not seem the type of woman to go around saying men were 'sweeties' or even agreeing they were.

"I followed Frank around the carriage and told him I did know where Dick had gone and in doing so accidently touched his arm."

"What happened then?"
"He fainted!"
"Understandable, I suppose, but hardly the image of a hardened criminal."
"I don't think he was really. He was just doing what Dick had told him to do. Apparently, they are brothers-in-law. Dick is married to Frank's younger sister."

"What did you do next?"

"Well, Punch must have heard Frank fall and came to see what had happened. For once I didn't know what to say. He asked me what happened to Frank and bent over him to see what was wrong."

Eva smiled one of her wicked grins. "I just tapped him on the shoulder and said 'it was their fault' and pointed to Peter and Paula who yet again went through their practiced routine of laughing their heads off!"

"Poor Frank and Punch." I did have some sympathy with what they had experienced. "Did he faint as well?"

"No, he just screamed and ran off down the road and we haven't seen him since! Do you want to see Peter and Paula's little routine?"

"No thanks. I think I have seen and heard enough. We ought to get on our way."

"Aren't you interested in how we got rid of the bodies?" I must have looked somewhat surprised. "Bodies?"

"Of Frank and Dick"

"I hope you are joking!"

"We tied Frank up in a similar manner to Dick and lifted them into the carriage. That took some doing."

"We all helped," explained Jacob.

Again Rebecca smiled and I wondered just what she was thinking. A little matter of a few weeks ago she and her two children were safe in Hampton Court

Palace and now they had been tying up criminals and lifting them into the back of a carriage! Not to mention the possibility of seeing ghosts laughing their heads off! I just hoped that their experiences at the hands of Eva would not damage them too much.

"We drove them to Bocardo Prison in Oxford. We had to ask for directions but it was near St Michael's Church so it wasn't too hard to find. Rebecca explained to the man there what had happened and he and some other men took them inside the prison."

Following the plotters' trail

As we slowly trotted out of the City of Oxford towards our next destination of Warwick, I decided to prepare for the future, as best I could, by reading the history book that Eva had been so shrewd in bringing. It had helped us before and maybe once again it could give us an insight into what lay ahead.

The book had said that after the failed attempt to blow up King James on 5th November 1605, Thomas Percy, Robert Catesby and the two Wright brothers had made their way to Holbeche House, which was supposed to be their 'safe-house' in Staffordshire.

For some reason, and the book wasn't clear on why, they decided to steal arms and ammunition including gunpowder from Warwick Castle. This seemed madness given that they were meant to be laying low for a time. One of the references to Thomas Percy said that when the plot was exposed early on

5ᵗʰ November 1605, Percy immediately fled to the Midlands, catching up with the others en route to Dunchurch in Warwickshire. Their flight ended on the border of Staffordshire at Holbeche House, where they were besieged early on 8ᵗʰ November by the pursuing Sheriff of Worcester and his men who were trying to locate the stolen arms and ammunition and apprehend the thieves that had taken them.

One other reference confirmed what we had heard previously from John Wright when we sat in Thomas Percy's house in Westminster. It said that John, along with his brother Christopher, originated from Plowland Hall in Welwick near Hull. He had been the third person to be initiated into the 'Gunpowder Plot'. Along with Thomas Wintour, he was given the task of officially telling Guy Fawkes of the conspirators' intentions to blow up the Houses of Parliament. At this point he removed his family from Twigmore Hall in Lincolnshire to a house belonging to Catesby at Lapworth in Warwickshire.

The book said :— 'On 4ᵗʰ November, the eve of the plot's discovery, John fled London with Catesby to take the news to Sir Everard Digby and the hunting party which had gathered at Coughton Court at Dunchurch in Warwickshire. Meeting several of their confederates, including Thomas Percy, on the way to the Midlands, their party eventually numbered almost 60 strong. After receiving Mass at Huddington Court on November 6ᵗʰ, they finally reached Holbeche House, the home of Stephen Lyttelton, in the late evening of 7ᵗʰ November. The conspirators by now were weary, and according to their confessions, had all but given up hope that their plans would succeed'.

The question was, 'would Thomas Percy take Grace with him to Dunchurch and then to Holbeche House or would he just flee London without her'? The thought of the latter made my heart sink. Without Grace the whole escapade would be, for me, a dangerous waste of time.

At least we might have two chances to meet her and try to persuade her to leave Percy and come with us back to where she rightly belonged in the twenty-first century. My ace card, if I was cruel enough to play it, was the following passage from the book:-

'Percy's flight ended with some of his fellow conspirators at about 10:00 pm on 7th November, at Holbeche House on the border of Staffordshire. He was unharmed by a gunpowder accident that injured Catesby and a few of the others, but those remaining resolved to stay and wait for the arrival of government forces, who were only hours behind. Thus at 11:00 am the following morning Richard Walsh, Sheriff of Worcester, and his company of 200 men besieged the house. In the ensuing firefight Percy was reportedly killed by the same musketball as Catesby, fired by a John Streete of Worcester. Christopher Wright was killed outright in the fight and his brother John was mortally wounded and died a few days later. The survivors were taken into custody and the dead buried near Holbeche, but on the orders of the Earl of Northampton, the bodies of Percy and Catesby were exhumed and their heads displayed on spikes at Westminster Palace'.

Of course, Grace might not believe or want to believe what the book said but it might be our only hope. She might even suffer the same fate as Percy at Holbeche House.

I decided to think about something else.

The forty mile or so journey from Oxford to Warwick took us through some of the most beautiful scenery in England, the Cotswolds. We made our way towards Banbury, the half-way point of our journey. I wasn't even sure if the famous 'Banbury Cross' of nursery rhyme fame would be there.

It wasn't! When I mentioned it to Rebecca, she said that she had heard that a lot of crosses that existed in towns had been destroyed five years earlier by Puritans in their attempt to remove all religious icons that the Catholics seemed to hold so dear. What a shame! I was certain someone had built another one in Banbury because I remembered driving past it!

At one of our stops on the six hour journey to Banbury we had discussed our plans.
"Jon thinks that he has found somebody who can help," said Eva.
"Who is it?"
"A lady called Margaret Carter. Jon is a very clever man and he has devised a plan for us to move forward in time."

"This should be very interesting!"

"Margaret was born on October 31st 1605 at a village called Southam not far from Dunchurch where Sir Everard Digby lives and more importantly where we hope Thomas Percy is taking Grace. She died in Bedford on January 18th 1645 after being accidently shot in a skirmish between the Roundheads and Cavaliers."

"Poor girl, but surely the drawback is that this Margaret whatever is still alive in 1605 and therefore not a ghost. So how is she going to be any use to us?"

"Ah well, that's where Jon has been really clever. The only way we can use Margaret is to go back to 2008!"

I must have looked a bit blank.

"Don't you get it, John? We use any old ghost to get us back to 2008 in the right spot to meet Margaret Carter in Southam and then use her to get to Bedford in 1645, which is not too far from Great Staughton Manor. Simple?"

"Just a minute. What do you mean by, 'use any old ghost'?"

"Well, Jon hasn't quite got all the pieces together but it shouldn't be too difficult for me to find a ghost in Southam to take us back to 2008."

"I hate to say it but this is beginning to make some sense. Let me get this straight. We go to Dunchurch, somehow kidnap Grace, find a ghost who can take us back to 2008 somewhere near Southam, find Margaret Carter and get her to transport us to near the place Valentine lived in 1645. On second thoughts it makes no sense at all."

"Why are you such a pessimist?"

"A realist, you mean."

"The real down-side to this is Jon will disappear from Limbo pretty soon and then we are all on our own again."

"Have you seen many ghosts on our travels? I have got out of the habit of asking."

"A few I suppose, but it is difficult to recognise them unless they have obvious injuries that killed them."

"Do you think that you will ever get used to living with the special powers you have?"
"It used to be fun and a novelty but now I wish it wouldn't happen. I've seen too many unpleasant sights that are hard to get out of my mind. Still we have had some fun times haven't we John and so there is no use me whinging on about it."

"I wouldn't call them 'fun times' but you have changed my life for ever and through you, I too, have seen things that I did not expect to see. The 17th century for one!"

"I hope that everything works out well for us and Grace too. I'd hate to think something awful would happen to her just because of what I did."
"Things sort of worked out OK last time so we need to stay positive."

"I like that, you finished up taking a mystery baby home to your wife and get arrested for kidnapping two children and you say things worked out OK?"

"Yes, I see your point, but if Jon's plan works we will be back in the good old 21st century and I can clear my name and live happily ever after, provided we can get Grace back with us!"

We explained Jon's plan, for what it was worth, to Rebecca and the children.
"What's going to happen to us when you disappear back home?" Rebecca said, "Can we come with you?"
I looked at Eva and she smiled.
"Of course you can, although you might find it a bit frightening at first. And you two," pointing at Charlotte and Jacob, "will have to go to school!"

The image was unimaginable but for the time being the children looked pleased as they would have Eva, their wonderful, mysterious and special friend.

We left Banbury, heading due north and, according to Jon, on a journey of fifteen or so miles towards Southam. Apparently we were on the Coventry road which was a busy link between there and Oxford. We passed a number of travellers heading in the opposite direction and for a time were part of a caravan of vehicles heading north.

I had decided, and Eva had agreed, that we had time to spend in the village of Southam in order to make ourselves familiar with some of the landmarks around the village which might help our search for Margaret in 2008. Of course the buildings and street layout would be vastly different but there might be something which might survive that would give us a reference point in our search. Eva thought that we might be able to track down Margaret's mother, but was Carter her maiden name or one she acquired through marriage?

Southam seemed a very pleasant little village which was situated on the banks of quite a wide river. Under Eva's (and presumably Jon's) orders we made our way past what looked like the Parish Church down to the river's edge where, yet again, we 'parked' up. Food was getting low so Rebecca and Charlotte went off in search of something to eat using the money we still had available from Anne Stow's generous gift. There was something that looked like a priory, similar to the one I had seen in Oxford and which had probably suffered the same fate at the hands of Henry VIII's dissolution of the monasteries.

That evening we sat down to the usual meagre meal of manchet bread, some early-season fruit and a watered down beer. The beer was, it was said, freer from health problems than the water. Seeing Charlotte,

Jacob and Eva sipping a weak form of alcohol, I had to smile thinking that in 400 years time it would be frowned upon.

We talked about our plans for finding Margaret's mother who would give birth in a few months time. Nothing concrete was decided but we had time on our side and with such a small village we were certain something would turn up to help us in our quest. The shops were probably the best place to start, but really we knew very little, only the fact that somewhere in the area there was a pregnant woman and that she was going to give birth to a baby girl on the 31st October and would name her Margaret.

Searching Southam

The parish church of St James had a spire and what looked like a new roof but the surprising thing was that this small place had its own Mint. It had, we were told, produced its own local currency for more than a hundred years because, apparently, the regular English currency was too high in value for everyday use. The Mint was a fine building almost rivaling the church in its décor. Obviously the village folk had readily accepted Rebecca's English currency, but somehow we needed to raise some local currency if we were to stay here for a couple of months.

Our random search tactics were not working. Our search for pregnant women was proving more difficult than we expected and even Rebecca's conversations with local women were not having much success.

May drifted into June and the evening light lengthened which, all told, made our time in Southam very pleasant. The weather had turned really warm and sunny and Eva tried to encourage Charlotte and Jacob not to play out in the sun for too long. I didn't have the heart to complain to Eva that she had forgotten the sun cream!

The money was running very low and one of our daily evening discussions turned to the problem of finding enough food to eat.

"I've had an idea," Eva said one evening. "We could start a school for young children and teach them to read and write. I got the idea because neither Jacob nor Charlotte have been taught to do either."

It wasn't such a bad idea. "But how will they pay us for something they might think they don't need?" Rebecca asked.

"In money or food. It might be that we just need to run a crèche."

"What is a crèche?" came Rebecca's inevitable question.

"Sorry," said Eva, "It's where we just look after the very young children and maybe play games so that their parents can go out and earn money."

I am not sure Rebecca had totally grasped the concept but nevertheless she sounded enthusiastic enough to give it a go.

"What could I do to help?"
"Well, John and I can do the teaching, and you could look after the young ones. You're a brilliant mother!"

The compliment came as something of a shock to Rebecca and she blushed.
"Yes, you are. You are brilliant!" repeated Charlotte and belatedly Jacob also added his praise for his mother.

"What are Jacob and me doing to help?"
You, my girl, are going to learn how to read and write," Eva said in a mock stern voice.
"Can I learn too?" Rebecca said quietly.
"Yes, of course. We can have a special evening class for you!"
"Thank you John that would be very kind of you."

We talked of our plans until the light faded and we retired to our individual sleeping areas.

We found out that the river we were camped by was called the River Stowe, which was quite apt given Jon's surname was one letter away. The locals simply called it 'The Brook'.

Our first problem was, how do we advertise our school? Eva soon realized that her plan of putting up notices in the village might not work, since very few villagers could read. The whole point of our school was to rectify that problem.

Initially Eva set about teaching Charlotte and Jacob the alphabet and then the usual practice of getting them to spell their names. With no writing implements, Eva resorted to using sand and dirt which was in plentiful supply by the side of the river. I helped or rather watched as this remarkable thirteen-year-old used all the skills associated with an experienced Primary School teacher to impart her knowledge of how you begin to learn to read and write. The thought did cross my mind that two children from the City of London might just finish up reading with a slight Yorkshire accent!

Rebecca thought that she could use her newly formed friendships in the village to encourage some children to come and try it. Free to all at first but with some small payment if they enjoyed it and their parents thought it was worthwhile. What surprised us was that after a little reluctance, mothers started to bring their children and stayed to watch. After a week or so we had two classes in the morning, one with children in, taken by Eva; and one for adults taken by yours truly! By lunch time the children had had enough and so too had the adults. The afternoons were given over to games such as, 'What time is it Mr. Wolf?' and 'hide and seek'. Eva was in her element and so too were the children. I only hoped that the games did not bring the children into contact with anything from the spirit world. It also gave Rebecca time to deal with Valentine and talk to the women about our search for Margaret's mum.

Slowly food and a little bit of local currency was passed to Rebecca who, for want of a better term, became the school secretary. After a time Eva decided to branch out with a little bit of arithmetic, and I followed suit with the adults. Not all the children and adults came everyday but there was a regular stream of those wishing to go to our school and with them came a regular stream of food and money.

On one of those beautiful sunny June mornings that seemed to have become few and far between in the 21ˢᵗ century, I found Eva looking unusually glum, sat at the water's edge.

"Not feeling too good this morning Eva?" I enquired.

"No, I am OK, but just had some bad news."

On the assumption that the news couldn't have come by mobile phone, I assumed this had something to do with the spirit world.

"Margaret doesn't exist?"

"No, it's not that. Jon has left Limbo. He said goodbye to me this morning. We are on our own now. I have to be honest and say that the idea for the school came from Jon. He was a really nice man and I shall really miss him."

"You might see him again when we get back. You could make it your mission to track down the ghost of Jon Stow. You know enough about him."

Malcolm J. Brooks

"Yes, you are right. Thanks John. Back to lesson preparation!"

"How are Charlotte and Jacob doing?"

"They are very good but they have a great teacher!" She smiled, got up and walked towards the coach.

With Jon gone, things were going to be a bit tricky but as the saying goes, 'always look on the bright side of life'. The brighter side of life arrived that morning as if by some miracle.

A very pasty-looking young woman approached the 'school' with a young girl of about six holding tightly to her hand. As usual in these cases the school secretary rose to meet her.

"Can we help you?" Rebecca enquired.

A softly spoken voice replied. "I arrived in the village a few days ago Ma'am and have nowhere to sleep and no food to eat. I have been watching you and wondered if you can help us."

"Where have you come from?"
"Warwick. I have disgraced my family and am with child, but the father of the child I am expecting is not my husband."
"What is your little girl called?"
"Letitia. She is named after my mother."
"And your name is?"
"Nancy. Nancy Carter."

192

"Just one moment please." Rebecca could hardly contain her excitement. She interrupted my lesson on subtraction. "Could I have a word with you John?"
"Excuse me." I said as I left my class of four adults.
"What is the matter?"
"I know it might not be who we are looking for but that lady over there is called Nancy Carter."
We looked at each other without saying a word and then we both smiled.
"Don't let her go anywhere."
"She wants food for her and her child."
"Then give her all we can spare."

I didn't say anything to Eva until we had finished morning lessons and most had departed for lunch. We didn't serve lunches and simply encouraged the 'pupils' to bring their own lunch or go home.

By the time Eva and I had finished for the morning, Rebecca was deep in conversation with Nancy, and Letitia sat snuggled into her mother's dress. They were both shabbily dressed and the young girl looked very frightened.

Eva held out her hand to Letitia but the young girl was not for moving. Even the arrival of Jacob and Charlotte did not loosen Letitia's grip on her mother.

After Nancy and Letitia had eaten all we could reasonably give them they departed. Nancy was very thankful for what we had given them but said that she did not want to be a burden on us and would find somewhere else to shelter for the night. Despite the pleas from Eva and Rebecca for them to stay, Nancy was adamant that she did not want to remain with us.

That evening, Rebecca gave us an account of the conversation that she had had with Nancy.

"I think that this is the lady we seek. She believes that her baby will be born in November. She hasn't thought of any names and I was careful not to suggest any. We want to be sure that this is she."

Rebecca said that Nancy was twenty-five years old but in a classic case of 'upstairs downstairs' she had been taken advantage of by her rich employer and had to leave the estate near Warwick in some disgrace.

"She is very pretty," said Eva.
"Yes, I can see why she might attract the attentions of her master," replied Rebecca.
"Maybe we could try and encourage her to stay with us. That would be alright wouldn't it John?"
"Yes, I suppose so. We might be able to encourage her to have the baby in a spot we can easily recognize in 2008."

"In the church!" suggested Eva.
"Not a bad idea."
"You cannot have a baby in a church," protested Rebecca.
"Can you have a baby in a field?" Eva asked Rebecca.
"Why yes many women have had their babies in the field in which they were working."

"I was thinking about these trees. That one looks as if it might last for another four hundred years," suggested Eva.

"I see what you mean. We would need a tree that is easily identifiable."

"I am not sure that the tree is a good idea. We had lots of storms last winter. Many trees were blown over," said Rebecca.

"In 1987 there is a great storm in the South of England," I added to confirm the riskiness of the 'tree' suggestion.

"OK," Eva said in a resigned voice indicating that her idea of selecting a tree and convincing Nancy that it would be a good place to give birth might just have a downside.

"What do you mean by 'OK', Eva? You use it a lot when you speak."

"Sorry, it must be a word invented some time after this century. It means 'everything is alright' but it is a strange thing when you think about it."

"Is it just two letters, an O followed by the letter K?"

"I think so. I never thought about it before. My mother sometimes says 'Okeydoke'."

Rebecca laughed, which caused Eva to do the same.

"You do talk in a funny manner, Eva."

"Yes I suppose I do. It's not Queen's English."

"You have another queen in 2008?"

"Yes we do and she is called Queen Elizabeth just like the one before King James, except of course she is Queen Elizabeth II. Does this mean you try and talk King's English?"

"No. He was born in Scotland and has an accent all of his own!"

The discussion about where we could encourage Nancy to give birth to Margaret came to a close with no resolution but with a decision to think about a possible place that might be easily recognizable. Every suggestion had its pitfalls but I liked Eva's idea of the church or near to it.

The school blossomed as June passed into July. Occasionally, the weather meant that school had to be abandoned and we had to huddle in the coach whist the storms passed by. But in general the weather was hot and sunny and ideal for a summer school by the banks of the River Stowe. It was for all of us a magical summer. The coins and food trickled in and kept us fed and watered and we became part of the village life.

We didn't see Nancy and Letitia every day but when they were hungry and needed company they would arrive at the 'coach school' as it became known.

Nancy was blossoming but had some of the health problems associated with being pregnant. The sight of her being physically sick was distressing for all of us but most of all for Letitia. Eva tried to reassure the young child that vomiting was part of the process of her mother having a baby and it would not last. The six-year-old was not convinced and clung onto her mother as she ejected the contents of her stomach.

For Nancy's part, she had been through it all before and also tried to alleviate Letitia's worries. Eva was beginning to weave her magic on Letitia and she began to join in the games that the younger pupils played most afternoons.

Southam had a 'holy well' on the bank of the River Stowe. Water from a natural spring fed this semi-circular well and the water poured through the mouth of some carved stone into the river. It was a great source of relatively healthy nourishment for Nancy and for the rest of us. Jacob had the job at break-time of filling the pots and pans we had acquired with the spring water and of returning them to the school for the pupils to drink from. He obviously enjoyed this manly role, requiring strength and agility in bringing the water back without spilling too much of it. Thus, he probably became the country's first school monitor!

In between teaching at the school during the morning and 'doing night-school' with Rebecca, I found enough time to read the 'history' book of the 17th century that Eva had had the foresight to bring. I was a bit careful not to let Rebecca see it as even though she wouldn't have been able to read it, some of the pictures were self-evident. She was well aware of the book and occasionally would ask me questions about what the future held.

"What happens in the Civil War?" she asked one afternoon as the children played.

I chose to read her a passage from the book rather than go into details about how the country was torn in two by the struggle between Royalists and those fighting on the side of the Parliament. I chose a couple of paragraphs relating to the village's role in the war.

"It says that King Charles I passed through Southam just before the outbreak of the Civil War and apparently was not made welcome by the townsfolk, who refused to ring the parish church bells. On 23rd August 1642, the day after King Charles I formally declared war on Parliament, a skirmish was fought outside the town between Parliamentary forces led by Lord Brooke and Royalist forces commanded by the Earl of Northampton. The Battle of Southam is claimed by locals to have been the first battle of the English Civil War. Later that year, Charles stayed in Southam before the Battle of Edgehill on 23rd October 1642. Later in 1645, Oliver Cromwell and 7,000 Parliamentary troops stayed in the town."

"Who was Oliver Cromwell?"
"He became known as the most notable leader of the Parliamentarian forces which opposed the King, but there were others before him who were as equally opposed to the King."
"I cannot believe that weak little Charles with all his ailments becomes King of England."
"I don't think Charles thought much about it or wanted it either."
"Henry did tease Charles so and was continually making fun of his little brother. We saw a lot of their

antics when we were at Hampton Court. Poor Henry. I did like him so. Does your book say much about him?"
"Do you really want to know?"
"Yes, please. I did love him so and he found time to come and play with all my children." Tears filled her eyes.

I found the appropriate bit and although I saved her from some of the more gruesome language, the tears started to flow.

"Little went right for King James in the years ahead. In 1612 Henry, the Prince of Wales, the paragon of Protestant patriots, lauded as virtuous, intelligent, handsome on a horse and refreshingly interested in those around him, died. The outpouring of sorrow at his huge funeral was genuine."

"It goes on to compare Henry with Charles. Do you want me to read on?"

"Yes, please. I want to know if they were accurate in what they recorded about the two boys."

"In contrast to the deceased Protestant hero, his replacement as Prince of Wales, Charles, had been such a puny child that no one expected him to survive infancy, and even at the age of five he needed to be carried around in people's arms. He was tongue-tied, solemn and very short. After Prince Henry died the golden suit of parade armour that had been made for him was passed down to the new Prince of Wales, but it was too big for him."

"That seems about right, but it is so unfair that they were so different. I did feel very sorry for little Charles."

History lesson over, we returned to the problem of where best to suggest Margaret be born.

"I have had a thought about that," said Rebecca, "There is a house next to St James' church. The elderly lady who lives there is a very kindly religious woman who perhaps might be persuaded to let Nancy have her baby there. I believe that she has been present at the births of many of the village's children."

"It certainly is a very good suggestion and provided that the church survives the next four hundred years it will be easy to find."

The birth of Margaret Carter

As the summer ended and the leaves started to turn in colour, the idyllic life-style we knew was about to come to an end. What was happening down at the Houses of Parliament was about to impinge on our wonderful 'summer school'.

The children of the village, including Jacob, Charlotte and Letitia, had a new village queen to follow in the footsteps of Queen Elizabeth. She dazzled them with her knowledge, her vitality but most of all her friendliness and compassion for all of them. They were all special to her and she was extra-special to them.

Eva had been very quiet about any spiritual activity that might be around the village and surely there were such activities in any community.

Rebecca brought us a bit of bad news.

"Nancy is thinking of leaving Southam and going to have her baby elsewhere. She thinks that people from Warwick will be out looking for her and doesn't want to be found."

"But we know that she has her daughter in Southam, because Jon said so," protested Eva.

"Despite the coincidence of the name, this still might not be the woman we want and also Jon could have got it wrong."

"You are a flaming pessimist, John!"

Before Rebecca could question Eva's use of the English language, I offered a clarification.
"By 'flaming' Eva doesn't mean that I ought to be burnt at the stake. It's just that in the 20th and 21st century some words are used to emphasize the meaning a little more."

Eva gave me one of her funny looks, then smiled as the penny dropped.
"Other words such as blinking, flipping and a few more I could mention are used to stress things but in themselves have no meaning."
Rebecca looked puzzled and I couldn't blame her. Lots of words we used in 2008 were just used for effect and had no meaning.
"I am looking forward to living in 2008!"
I gave Eva a glance that was meant to say 'that cannot happen', but she just shrugged and said, "Yes it will be fun for you."

As 31ˢᵗ October approached, Nancy looked as if she was having twins. The saying 'couldn't fall flat on her nose', was certainly true. But she was in good spirits, was eating and drinking well and as far as we could tell, everything was going according to plan.

Rebecca had convinced Nancy that she and Letitia were better off hiding in the coach during the day and going for a 'waddle' at night. She had kept herself to herself as the saying goes and had not spent too much time associating herself with the other villagers.

The nights began to draw in and the light started to fade in the very early evening. It was a golden October and the benefit of that month was the harvest. Fruit, particularly apples, were in abundance and the fees for 'autumn school' were raised not by us but by the villagers who had a little more to spend or give. Some of the youngsters (and the adults) were becoming reasonable readers, although writing without pens was more of a challenge. But given the challenges that we faced I think Ofsted would have given us 'excellent' for our sheer inventiveness. Eva had scrounged some flat pieces of wood that acted as trays and then filled them with a combination of dirt and sand so the children could write in them and with one quick shake have a clean slate to write again. The occasional accidental shaking of the trays was an occupational hazard!

Those of us who understood what was about to happen, all started to feel a little nervous. The plan was so fragile that any number of things could go wrong.

The one thing that had gone right, however, was that Rebecca had persuaded old Mrs Evans that Nancy could give birth in her home and she would help with the delivery. The thing that was wrong was that on October 30ᵗʰ there was no sign of Nancy going into labour. I am not the best at relating these matters but at school that day everything started very normally. I recall Nancy going for her usual 'waddle' in the late afternoon with Letitia and Rebecca at her side. I realize the term 'waddling' is a little unkind, particularly coming from a man who has never experienced pregnancy but it did sum up the motion that took place.

Although she probably had a very uncomfortable night, Nancy still seemed to have no signs of going into labour and in her mind the birth was not due until November. So here was Hallowe'en with no 'trick or treaters' knocking at our coach door. I wasn't too sure whether this pagan festival would be celebrated. Had pumpkin lanterns been invented?

The dark mornings meant that school had to start a little later, but now even Letitia was quite keen on her lessons with Eva, and so she left her mother in the coach to walk the short distance to where Eva sat waiting for her class to assemble.

Suddenly we all heard a loud gasp followed by a distressingly agonizing groan coming from inside the coach. This was not dissimilar to the sound that someone might make when hitting their thumb with a hammer. All of us ran to the coach where Nancy lay. The scene was not very dignified for poor Nancy. Eva said that she would fetch Mrs Evans. The plan to take Nancy to her house might not now be operational.

Nancy's waters had already broken. Whether she had been having contractions before this nobody knew as she had said little about how she felt. I suppose she didn't want to be a burden on us, when in truth, she was being a life-line. A shocked Letitia had jumped up into the coach and looked frightened at what she saw. She resumed what had been her natural position beside her mother, tears in her eyes at her mother's obvious distress.

Things seemed to calm down a little and Rebecca took control. I wondered if I would be asked to fetch water and towels, in other words get the man well out of the way.

After ten minutes or so Mrs Evans arrived travelling as fast as she could given her age, with Eva trotting beside her. She puffed and panted as she approached the coach. Inside I could hear moans periodically coming from Nancy.

Mrs Evans asked Letitia to leave her mum. She refused. Eva stepped up on the coach's steps and whispered in Letitia's ear. Slowly Letitia got up from beside her mother and climbed down from the coach with Eva.

Mrs Evans and Rebecca had a brief discussion and must have decided that when the time was right they would help take Nancy to Mrs Evans' home. The coach could be used to transport her most of the distance.

Rebecca asked me if I could fetch the horses that were tethered a short distance away and couple them to the coach ready for departure.

After arriving at Mrs Evans' home and helping Nancy into the house, Eva and I returned the coach to its original position and continued with school. One of Eva's jobs was to take Letitia's mind off the birth of her sister. She must have done a brilliant job because by the end of morning school Letitia was absorbed in some game with Charlotte, Jacob and Valentine. Letitia was quite taken with Valentine probably because he was the only one younger than she was, so she too could assume the role of a 'teacher'. Valentine, despite his limited chances to do so, was able to run rather unsteadily, much to the amusement of Letitia who was cast in the role of 'chaser' in the game they were currently playing.

Once all the other children and adults had departed for lunch, the five of them returned to the coach for their lunch of apples and bread, which was becoming something of a favourite of mine. One of the upsides of the 17th century diet was that I had lost weight.

Jacob assumed his manly duty of fetching water from the spring.

"What is happening to my mam?" eventually came the inevitable question from Letitia.

"Eva was quick to respond. "She is going to bring you a little sister and you will be able to play with her."

Letitia's eyes lit up at the thought of having someone to play with permanently.

"Shall I go and see what is happening?" said Eva.

"Not yet. It takes quite a time for these things to happen and we know it will be before the day is out. When you have finished eating, go and play some games before it gets dark. It won't be too long."

They all ran off to resume whatever game they had been playing. Eva barking out instructions and, as ever, being leader of the pack.

Whilst there was still light and nothing much else for me to do, I took out the history book and read the bit about what was happening in London at this very time.

Under the heading of 'The Monteagle Letter' I read the following passage:-

'On Saturday 26th October 1605 Monteagle received an anonymous letter while at his house in Hoxton, warning him to stay away from Parliament. Uncertain of its meaning he delivered it to Salisbury, who before he received the letter was already aware of certain stirrings, although he did not then know the exact nature of the plot or who exactly was involved. Rather than inform the king he decided to wait, to see how events unfolded. Catesby's reaction was somewhat different; he and Wintour suspected Tresham was the letter's author and went to confront him. Tresham managed to convince the pair of his innocence, all the while urging them to abandon the plot. Percy reacted to the news by declaring that he was still ready to go ahead with the plot and he visited the infant Prince Charles on 1ˢ November, indicating perhaps that some rearrangement of the plan was being considered and that the Prince was to be kidnapped. A statement by one of the servants claimed that he visited the prince's lodgings, and "made many enquiries as to the way into his chamber".

Percy and a mysterious woman visited the Earl of Northumberland on 4ᵗʰ November, at Syon House, west of London. It was suggested that his visit was a "fishing expedition", to find out what, if anything, Northumberland had heard about the letter. It would later prove disastrous for the Earl, who claimed that there was nothing treasonable about their conversation, and that Percy had merely asked him "whether he would command any service" before leaving. Percy then went to another of Northumberland's properties, Essex House in London, and spoke with his nephew, Josceline. Later that evening he met with Wintour, John Wright and Robert Keyes and assured them that all was well, before heading to his lodgings at Westminster, where he left orders for his horses to be made ready for an early departure the next morning for the home of Sir Everard Digby'.

I found myself muttering, 'please bring the mysterious woman with you'.

Later that evening Margaret Carter was born into the world as predicted and in a place that should be easy to find.

Coughton Court

We left Southam on a very rainy 'All Saints Day', 1ˢᵗ November, and headed for Coughton Court, the present home of Sir Everard Digby. According to the locals Dunchurch was about ten miles away from Southam. Although Letitia was sad to see Eva and the other children leave, it was more than compensated for by the fact that she now had a baby sister and also that her mother had come through the ordeal satisfactorily.

"Are we certain that Thomas Percy will bring your friend with him?" Rebecca asked as we sat in the pouring rain guiding the horses along a muddy track.
"No we are not certain he will. However he seems to have prepared himself for his escape out of London, so I am hopeful that his preparations included Grace. He seems to be a ladies' man so I am hoping he cannot do without the company of a woman."

"He doesn't seem to be a very nice man, this Thomas Percy."

"No, he isn't, but he does meet with quite a tragic death."

"Is it good having a book that tells you the future?"

"No, not really. I certainly wouldn't like someone coming from the future telling me what was going to happen and how I was going to die."

"Do you have astrologers like Simon Foreman in London who claim to be able to predict the future? I have seen him at the Palace on a number of occasions."

"Yes, in 2008 there are many people who claim to have the power to see into the future. The bible is often used in this way as well to predict the end of the world! I am sure there are lots of things we don't know in 2008, just like you don't know about computers, cars, trains, televisions and airplanes."

"Such strange words! Would it be hard for you to explain what each one is?"

The explanations took a long time, but Rebecca seemed keen to hear about the strange world of 2008. She asked quite a few questions which showed that I had taken a lot of things for granted.

How does such a heavy object, with lots of people in, stay in the sky?
How can computers 'talk' to each other when they are only made of metal?

Rebecca had an intelligent and inquisitive mind but her talk of visiting 2008 was worrying.

By early afternoon, with the rain still falling, we arrived at Coughton Court. It had a long driveway in wonderful countryside with cattle and sheep on both sides of the road. The house was very large and symmetrical in shape and beige in colour, no doubt made of local stone from around the Cotswold area. It had a castellated central frontage which was obviously the main entrance and it had three floors. It had two identical 'wings', also castellated, with large windows both upstairs and down. There were symbols all around the walls, presumably had some religious significance. Above the upstairs windows were what looked like very small windows which on closer inspection could best be described as clover-shaped crosses.

Surprisingly, we were not impeded in our approach to the house until we were quite close, when two uniformed men, who presumably had been tracking our route through the grounds, came out to meet us. Both were armed.

The one advantage that we had was knowledge. Knowledge of what was about to happen, which gave us power. Sir Everard would be expecting some Catholics fleeing from London even if the 'Gunpowder Plot' had succeeded and such people would have servants and children that would need to be moved to a safer area than London was going to become.

The question was what was the most convincing tale to tell? At one of our stops on the journey we had decided on a safe approach. We would pretend to be the family and servants of Thomas Percy's new love, Grace Collin. Since Sir Everard would not be too familiar with Thomas' new girlfriend, we would not be so likely to say something that would arouse suspicion. We thought that even if Sir Everard wanted to check our story, it would be a couple of days before he could contact Thomas and he probably had other more pressing things on his mind. We knew enough about Thomas Percy to convince him that our 'mistress' was his!

I left it up to Rebecca to explain to the guards who we were and although we were not allowed immediate entrance into the inner courtyard, eventually we were waved through.

A gentleman who introduced himself as Colin Richards and who claimed to be Sir Everard's right-hand-man, possibly, in truth, his butler, came out of the main entrance of the house to meet us in the courtyard.

"Sir Everard is not available at the moment. He is away on some business."

We probably knew what that business might entail but chose to remain silent on the matter.

"Would it be possible to rest our coach and horses in the parklands and then we will be no inconvenience to you or his Lordship, whilst we wait for our mistress?"

Rebecca's shrewd assessment of the situation and raising Everard to a Lord seemed to do the trick.

"Yes, I will get one of the gardeners to show you a place where you can stay until Sir Everard returns."

A strongly-built young man was summoned and given instructions on where we should put the coach and horses and since no offer of a bed was made, where we would spend the night.

We probably could have just parked the coach somewhere close by but felt that from the grounds we could watch the comings and goings and hopefully see Grace and Thomas arrive.

As soon as it was mentioned to Grace that her family and servants were here, it would be up to her what she did. We were relying on her not to give the game away and come and see what we were up to, rather than suggesting that we were Protestant spies. At that point I would have to produce the book and show her what destiny held for Thomas Percy and possibly for her.

There were to be lots of comings and goings during the evening, with Catholics fleeing London and meeting up at the house. Although we had met John Wright and Percy only Eva had met the likes of Catesby and the rest of the conspirators.

Somehow we needed to speak to Grace and convince her that if she didn't come with us, there was a strong possibility she could die in a few days' time.

The book seemed to suggest that Thomas Percy would arrive with Catesby and the two Wright brothers on the 5th November, and from what the gardeners had said there was to be a hunting party on the 4th November. Presumably this was some sort of cover-up for lots of people arriving at the house at that time.

All we could do was sit and wait.

There was one other thing that Eva could do. If all went to plan we would need to transport Eva, Valentine and myself back to 2008. To do this she needed a friendly ghost whose 'corridor of transit' would take us back close to Southam but in the year 2008 or was it 2009 now? I had completely lost track of dates. Time seemed to run evenly in the two centuries last time we visited, but the times of the 'corridors of transit' seemed to move time around depending on the ghosts' dates of birth and death. We simply needed to get back to the modern times we had left!

Rebecca, Charlotte and Jacob were another problem that Eva and I had to face. To take them with us would be, I was certain, a shock to their systems. From the relative peace and quiet of the 17th century to the noise of the 21st would have a great effect on the two children as well as their mother. Maybe now was the time to discuss the plans in more detail with Rebecca and the children spelling out in no uncertain terms the dangers of what we were doing. The choice would be theirs.

When I spoke to Eva about the matter the following morning, she had a completely different viewpoint.

"Charlotte and Jacob would love to be with us in 2008. There is so much more to do than here. Their lives are so boring here."
"But look what they would have to do. They have never been to school and they would be so far behind that they would never catch up."

"You could teach them John. A lot of what we are taught in school is rubbish and useless. When am I ever going to use Algebra? Why do I need to know about the Romans or why Hitler started the war? And what is Shakespeare all about, he cannot write proper English? You could teach them what they need to know to get by!"

This was an emotional, passionate Eva, the likes of which I had never heard before. I could have made an attempt to answer each of her questions and, if time allowed, even made a plan for her to meet Shakespeare; he must have been around somewhere close by, maybe in Stratford.

"We will have a word with Rebecca and the children and leave the decision to them."

As the morning of 4th November 1605 dawned, we had counted that about fifty people had arrived at the

216

house for the so called 'hunting party'. Bearing in mind what was going to happen at Holbeche House in four days' time, the term seemed appropriate. I had no intention in subjecting Rebecca and the children to that massacre. It was here and now or nowhere. Grace had to see sense despite what her feelings for Thomas Percy were.

It was one of those murky November mornings where the mist hangs around all day. It was a day for playing with conkers, and they were at the heart of the game that the children were playing, as ever led by Eva and her imagination. The giant horse chestnut tree that we were sheltering under had dropped dozens of conkers with their green spiky overcoats and the children had great delight in smashing these open to reveal the shiny brown gem that lay within. The delight of generations of boys and girls was there in a nutshell and the collection of them transcended time. The game seemed to involve a kind of 'pétanque' where the object was to get the conker you threw as near to the wheel of the coach as you could. The horses were in no danger of these flying objects as they were busy grazing thirty metres or so away. Squeals of delight as success followed a good or lucky throw. Even Valentine was joining in, although the direction of his throw was not as predictable as those of the other three. Of course, Eva was the arbiter of the winner.

Suddenly, Rebecca said, "There is someone approaching," and pointed towards the house. Sure enough a man was striding purposefully towards us. Had our story been uncovered as the lie it was?

It was Colin. He was a man of great stature. He was over six feet tall with a broad chest. It was difficult to gauge his age but he was at least forty years old. We knew Grace hadn't arrived yet. If she was to arrive at all, it would be tomorrow. Maybe a messenger had been sent to say she had no family or servants.

"Good day," he said in a very hearty friendly manner, "Sir Everard would like to meet you if you would care to follow me to the house."
"All of us?" I enquired.
"Well you and your good lady."
I chose not to correct him. The least we said about ourselves the better.
"We must just make sure that the children are alright and then we will come along."

He hovered for a while but then turned and started to walk back to the house.

"We will be with you in a moment."
"What's all this about?" said Eva when Colin was out of earshot.

"I'm not sure but we must be careful what we say. You will be alright staying here, won't you, looking after the others?"

Eva beckoned me to one side. "Could you see the man who was standing by Colin's shoulder and who is still watching us from over there?"
"No, I can't.'

"Thought as much. He seems too scruffily dressed to be a member of the posh household staff like Colin. I wonder what he wants. Of course, he thinks we cannot see him." She took my arm so I could see the man for myself.

"What do you think we should do?"
"I think that it would be a good thing for me to have a word with him before you visit Sir Everard."
"I'll wait here and have a word with Rebecca about what we can and cannot say in front of Sir Everard."

Eva walked away towards the man who was in for a bit of a shock!

For some moments she stood looking up and talking and it was evident to anyone who knew of Eva's powers what she was doing. She wasn't mad and talking to herself or on her 'hands free' mobile phone. She was conversing with a ghost.

We all watched what, for us, was a one-sided conversation. After about ten minutes, Eva returned.

"I think that they may have sussed who we are."
"What do you mean by 'sussed', Eva?"
"Sorry," said Eva, "I meant that I think Sir Everard knows that we are not the family of Grace Collin."

"What did the man have to say?"
"Part of it was what we already knew, that this is a meeting of Catholics who are hoping to seize power once King James is dead. Blown up, they hope, by

gunpowder in Westminster. They are suspicious of us turning up at this time and they are all armed."

"Does he have suggestions as to what we can do to escape?"

"He does actually. He says that with my powers he can transport us into a hiding place within the house."

"Why would he want to help us?" asked Rebecca.

"Apparently he is not too keen on his ex-master Sir Everard Digby. Blames him for his death. Something to do with faulty machinery."

"Do you trust him or is he leading us into a trap?"

"Well, if you can hang on, sorry, wait a few minutes I can find out."

"How?"

"Never you mind. I will be back shortly. Stay here and don't go into the house. Put the children into the coach and wait." Eva was very forceful when she wanted to be. Rebecca and I looked at each other, shrugged our shoulders and did as we were told. Eva walked back to where presumably the man was standing and then as if in a puff of smoke, disappeared.

"Where did Eva go?" asked a startled Charlotte.

"She has just gone to see if everything is safe for us to stay here, darling." Rebecca replied reassuringly.

It was one of those moments when time passed incredibly slowly, like waiting for the kettle to boil. It seemed like an age. With probably the exception of Valentine who was busy building a castle of conkers, we were all worried by Eva's prolonged absence. Without Eva we were in desperate trouble. Maybe, I should not have let her go alone. Fleeing was our last option.

After some time, a slightly less hospitable Colin arrived wanting to know why we were keeping his master waiting. It was very rude of us.

Rebecca was quick off the mark. "We seem to have lost one of the children. Eva, our oldest girl has gone missing and we have been trying to find her. Please apologize to Sir Everard and say that we will come to the house as soon as we have found Eva."

A slightly disgruntled Colin once again set off back towards the house empty-handed, probably fearing the wrath of his master.

"Well done, Rebecca."

"It's what a mother thinks of when one of her children goes missing. I was not telling a lie. We don't know where she is!"

"Do you think that we ought to pretend to be looking for her?"

But before we could start our mock search, out of the trees bounced Eva. We couldn't tell if there was anyone with her, but she looked really hyped-up as if she had had an exciting experience.

In a slightly breathless voice she said, "There's a priest hole in the house in which we can hide but more importantly my friend Tom here can get us back to the 21st century here in Dunchurch. All we need once we have got Grace is a bus ride to Southam."

"A bus ride?"

"I'll explain later," I replied to Rebecca's predictable question, "We need to move the coach out of sight as if we have left. We don't need it any more but we don't want them searching for us in the house."

"Is the priest hole big enough for all six of us?"

"Well, I wouldn't want to stay in it for weeks but just for a day it is an ideal place for Tom and me to keep an eye on who is arriving. He seems very keen to help."

"What if Valentine cries?"
"I hadn't thought of that!"
"Maybe there is a way of dealing with that. Do you suspect your friend Tom has a good motive for helping us?"

Suddenly a branch was blown off one of the trees we were standing near and hit me full in the face, knocking me to the ground.

"I think that was Tom's answer to your untrusting remark. Remember he can see and hear everything we do."

"And throw branches." I said as I regained my feet and wiped a small amount of blood from my lip, "Sorry Tom!"

"What were you going to say about a way of dealing with the situation?"
"Well I could take Valentine and the coach and horses some distance away. As I said we don't need them anymore. We could stay there until morning and walk back and with the help of you and Tom, join you in the priest hole. Have we any food left?"

"A little," said Rebecca.
"Well, you take that for the night and I will find something for Valentine and me. Tomorrow night we could be back where we belong having a burger at McDonalds!"

Before Rebecca could respond, I added, "It's made out of meat of some sort and made in a shop started by an American."
I looked at Rebecca and she pulled a face that said, 'I still don't understand'.
Eva laughed and said, "Your explanations are more pathetic than mine!"

Rebecca collected all that she thought they would need from the coach and warned Charlotte and Jacob that they must be quiet whilst in the house. What she did not warn them about was the walk into a 'corridor of transit' which was quite an experience but one which they may have to do quite a few times in the next day or two.

Within minutes the four (or was it five?) of them disappeared, leaving poor Valentine a bit perplexed. I picked him up and we made our way to the horses. I sat him on Bits (or was it Bobs?) and he hung on for dear life although I had one hand firmly clasped on his clothing.

Having harnessed the two horses to the coach and with Valentine happily sat on my knee, we made our way out of the extensive grounds of Coughton Court and towards the village of Dunchurch.

The Gunpowder Plot explosion

After a fairly restless night brought about by the cold, Valentine crying and my foreboding of what was to happen, the morning of the 5th November 1605 dawned. What was going on elsewhere was going to have an effect on people for centuries. The sad thing was that for centuries to come people would also die because of what was happening on this day. There had been too many accidents over the years resulting in the death and maiming of children because of Bonfire Night and the associated so-called, 'mischief night' that preceded it.

On the plus side 'Bonfire Night' or as my son had mistakenly called it when he was young, "Bunfire Night', did bring much pleasure and community spirit at the gatherings to celebrate this misadventure. A friend of mine was almost hit by a misdirected rocket that smashed into a window close by. He managed to jump out of the way but sadly for him he jumped headlong into a garden pond.

Most people looked forward to the celebration but I wasn't looking forward to what was going to happen on this day. There were too many things that could go wrong.

I reasoned that if Thomas and Grace were setting off from Westminster early this morning, riding on horseback and catching up with Robert Catesby and his party they would probably be at Coughton Court sometime in the mid-morning.

The morning was cold but quite bright and the rain of the previous few days had abated. I really enjoyed the leisurely stroll that Valentine and I had as we walked the two or so miles back to our rendezvous point with Eva and Tom. Of course, Valentine couldn't walk it all and for periods of time we had rests and I did a bit of carrying.

It took us a little longer than I expected, but I was in no hurry. As we neared the house I could see a number of carts carrying barrels and what looked like ammunition and rifles being transported up the drive. These must have been some of the stolen items that eventually would lead to the tracking down and killing of those involved in the plot. Why on earth would you want to steal gunpowder and ammunition from a place as famous as Warwick Castle at a time when you were supposed to be lying low so you could not be found? I think that it only served to show the desperation and fanatical characters of the men involved in the plot.

As I stood there, with Valentine in my arms, I couldn't help thinking about what he might be able to remember of his bizarre life so far. He had had a massive effect on the lives of so many people and yet probably would not remember any of them.

I was snapped out of my thoughts by the arrival of twenty or so people on horseback. They were riding quickly up the long drive to the house. It seemed that most of them had discarded their cloaks, presumably to increase their speed of travel. It certainly was cold enough for them to have worn them. At the back of the column was the noticeable figure of a woman. Surely, it had to be Grace?

The riders were met by a flurry of men ready to take their horses to the stables. They dismounted and all headed for the house.

After about thirty minutes in which Valentine and I played conkers I saw Eva appear from behind the same trees as before. I stood up and waved. She came running over.

"She's here! Grace is here with Thomas."
"I don't suppose that you have had time to talk to her."
"No. They've only just arrived."
"Is everything OK with Rebecca and the children?"
"Yes, they are fine, if a bit cramped."
"Have you managed to find anything out?"

"Yes. Quite a bit. Sir Everard is quite a nice person and he has a lovely wife, Mary and two children. One has a real funny name, Kenelm and he is about Valentine's age and Mary has just given birth to a second son called, have a guess?"

"This is all very interesting but of no use to us."
"He is called John!" she said ignoring my comment.
"Have we any useful information?"
"Oh yes, they are staying the night here and moving on tomorrow. I think everybody is leaving for various places to hide. The 'Gunpowder Plot' failed you know!"

"You don't say! Well, we would have been celebrating the wrong thing for all these years if it had succeeded. What do you know!"
"Is that sarcasm? I thought teachers weren't supposed to use sarcasm."
"Only in the classroom! Now let's get on with finding and talking to Grace."
"Tom and I managed to look around most of the house. It was difficult because there are so many people in the house, sleeping all over the place."

BOOM, BOOM! There were two large explosions from within the house.

"What was that?" asked Eva.
"I think I know. It mentioned the explosions in the book but didn't say where it took place."
"What explosions?"

"You are not going to believe this but all that gunpowder they stole got wet in all the rain we have had and so they decided to dry it out by the fire!"

"You have got to be joking!"

"Nope. That's what has just happened. One person loses his sight and Robert Catesby and others are quite badly hurt."

"What about Grace . . . and Rebecca and Charlotte and Jacob?"

"Well Rebecca, Charlotte and Jacob should be alright. It is only the people in the room with the gunpowder that are the ones to get hurt. If my memory serves me well, according to the book, Thomas Percy does not get injured and if Grace is with him neither should she."

"We need to take a look. Come with me."

"What about Valentine?"

"He can come too. There is one young boy in there so he shouldn't be too conspicuous. Come on!"

I picked up a surprised Valentine and followed Eva towards the trees and presumably Tom who was waiting there.

As we have done a number of times previously, Eva and I held hands with Valentine in my arms and walked towards Tom. The bright tunnel lay ahead. As usual, I could neither see nor feel anything. A strange sensation swept through my body. After a few moments I found myself in what I assumed was a priest hole.

Rebecca, Charlotte and Jacob looked relieved to see us.

"Did you hear those explosions?" Rebecca asked.
"Yes we did. Please stay here a little bit longer while Eva and I go and find Grace.

We exited the priest hole and there was smoke and confusion everywhere. I still was amazed that an intelligent man would choose to use a fire to dry gunpowder. They obviously had not been to a Bonfire Night!

We passed several people whom we did not recognize and fortunately in the confusion they did not bother with us.

"I know it might be dangerous because of other explosions but let's go to the room where the explosions took place." Eva's suggestion sounded all wrong but maybe she had some insight into what had happened.

It was obvious which room had taken the force of the explosions. There were debris and bodies all over it. There were still cries for help coming from people with horrendous burns. Some bodies were motionless, but we could hear the distinct cry of a female voice. It could be that of Mary, Sir Everard's wife or any of the servants.

"It's Grace. She's over there!"

She looked in a really bad way and was barely conscious. Thomas was noticeable by his absence. If he had really loved Grace he would have sought her out as we did. The book said that he was uninjured by the blasts, so where was he?

"Grace, Grace, it's Eva and John. Are you ok?"

She was badly burned down the left side of her face. Her prettiness had gone. I removed small pieces of debris from around her legs. It wasn't obvious whether she had sustained any more injuries. There were unlikely to be any broken bones, unless the blast had thrown her against something in the room.

"Eva, I need you to go get Rebecca and the children and meet me out at the front of the house with Tom. Quick, I need to get her out before anyone sees us."

Eva disappeared and I slowly moved Grace into a position so that I could pick her up. I could see that fragments of her skin had moulded themselves into the dress she was half-wearing. She groaned.

"Sorry," I said instinctively and tried my best to gently put her over my shoulder. She screamed and then went quiet. Hopefully she had fainted. I exited the room without really knowing where I was going. Logic said to head for any daylight I could see. The smoke and dust were beginning to settle. I bumped into a man who lay on the floor.

"It's me Robert Catesby. I'm badly injured. Please help me!"

"Sorry Robert, I am not a doctor but I need to get this lady to one very quickly."

My comment may have been something of a mystery to him had he been in the mood for chatting. I could smell fresh air and appeared to be going in the right direction. I entered what must have been a large entrance hall with many large paintings adorning the walls. Strange as the thought was I recognized this hall and was sure I had been here before. I headed for where I believed the door to the outside courtyard was situated and sure enough there it was. Grace still wasn't making any sound. Once in the courtyard I could see clearly and more importantly I could see the trees that I needed to reach. Even though Grace was slim and probably only seven or eight stone, her weight was beginning to be a problem.

Outside the courtyard I had to put her down on the grass. Someone tapped me on the shoulder and I swung around expecting the worst. It was John Wright, the boy from East Yorkshire.

"Can I help you?"

I looked at the kind young man who was to die in three days time and said, "Yes please I am trying to get Grace to safety by those trees over there."

"Don't I know you from somewhere?" he asked.

"Yes, I think we have met before, but I can't remember where," I lied.

He helped me pick Grace up and between us we carried her to the trees where I hoped Eva would be waiting.
"You need to go back to the house. Robert Catesby is badly injured and needs help quickly."

And with that the good hearted John turned and ran back to the house. It was a very sad moment. I could have said, 'Please don't go to Holbeche House. Stay with us and go back to Twigmore House and the beautiful rhododendrons that have been planted there in the woods that surround your home.' But we all have a fate and his was to die at Holbeche House.

Eva's voice snapped me out of my malaise. "Over here. Let's go!"

At the same moment I heard a loud voice from the house, "Hey you man, leave that girl alone!" He started to run towards us. I had no option. I threw Grace over my shoulder. She murmured which was a good sign. I grabbed Eva's hand and like a daisy chain she held Charlotte's hand, she in turn held Jacob's, he was holding his mother's, and she had Valentine on one arm. We ran in this strange fashion towards Tom and the bright light appeared once more.

Rebecca's horror

The sun shone brightly and as I looked around at the horror struck faces that surrounded us, I was at a loss for words. It took some minutes to gather my thoughts and then a woman screamed. It was Grace. The extent of her burns was now obvious and the hot sunshine was doing them no good at all.

There were lots of people walking on the grass on which we all sat, all of them dressed in strange costumes

"We're back in 2008 John!"
"We need to get Grace to a hospital as soon as possible!" I ran to the nearest person.
"Could I borrow your phone to dial 999. My friend has been horribly burned and we need to get her to a hospital."

Reluctantly, the lady delved into her handbag and handed me her phone.

The ambulance arrived in little more than fifteen minutes. Fifteen minutes of real agony for Grace. We had managed to move her out of the sun and into the stately home that all these people were visiting. It suddenly dawned on me that this was the same Coughton Court that we had just left in 1605 but without the devastation. Clearly someone had fixed the problem in the intervening years.

There were staff at the house who were very good and some had medical knowledge but I was really happy when the Paramedics arrived. We all knew that the questions about how Grace had received the injuries would be difficult to answer. Instantaneous sunburn of that degree did not exist, well not in England in 2008.

As you might imagine we were getting some strange looks but funnily enough not as many as you would expect. Eva worked it out first.

"This is one of those houses run by the National Trust. They must think we are part of the exhibit, dressed in period costume!"

I had to smile but it didn't last for long. Grace was our first priority. The lady Paramedic asked me how the injuries occurred. I had to be honest because it might affect the treatment they would give her.

"There was an explosion of gunpowder, and Grace was caught in the blast."

She looked around at her male companion and the look was clear, 'this man must be on something'.

Eva tried to help, "It's true. We can explain but it will take some time."
"I realize it must be difficult for you but all we ask is that you get her to hospital as soon as possible."

They took down our names and other details. With any luck by the time they had been checked we would be on our way back to the 17th century.

They asked me to go with them to the hospital but I declined saying I had four children to look after. After some debate they decided that Grace was their priority. I gave them my true mobile and home numbers. From memory my mobile was in some prison near York, but it would ring if they rang it. It would be answered by a prison warder and that would be one interesting conversation as would the one with my wife Ann if they decided to phone home.

All that explanation was for the future. As the ambulance left, I looked around for Rebecca and the children. They hadn't followed us into the house but were still sat on the grass where we had arrived.

Rebecca looked traumatized and both children were clutching at her in fear.

"What is the matter?" said Eva as we approached.
"It's so different, it's frightening. The noise is deafening!"

There must have been a main road nearby and of course airplanes occasionally flew overhead. It is surprising what level of background noise you get used to, piped music, cars, etc.

Suddenly a brass band started up which made us all jump.
It suddenly occurred to me that we had no money.
"How are we going to get to Southam with no money?"
Eva smiled and said, "Stay here I won't be long."

"Are those the cars you talked about? They travel very fast."
"They can go a lot faster!" It probably wasn't a helpful comment.

"Let's go and find somewhere quieter."

But the children were mesmerized by the music coming from the brass band.

"Do you want to go closer to have a look?"
"No, we are as you say OK here."

A little girl came running up to play with Valentine who was happily playing in some dirt he had found. She turned to Jacob and in a very eloquent voice said, "Are you part of the display?"

Jacob looked horrified. He did not understand what he had been asked. She repeated the question and I answered, "Yes we are. We are modeling the costumes from the 17th century." She seemed happy with this and sat down to join Valentine in the dirt.

"Olivia, come here. Don't play in that soil. Do you want an ice cream?"
At this the girl was up and gone.

It was some time before Eva returned and I was beginning to feel really sorry for Rebecca and the children. They certainly were 'fish out of water'.

When she arrived she had a big smile on her face.
"OK what have you been up to?"
"Getting us some money!" She held out her hand in which there must have been a hundred pounds.
"Where did you get that sort of money? You haven't stolen it have you?"

"Well, not exactly. I used my brain. My mother is always watching those antique programmes and old things sell for lots of money. So when we were in the house in 1605 I borrowed a few small items. You know some spoons etc. Anyway I think they have got a bargain. They were very suspicious at first. Thought I'd stolen them from the house now but they soon checked and realized that they had nothing like the things I was showing them. It could be a good business for me in the future. Pop back in time and acquire a few things from history and sell them to the

National Trust or at an auction. Now all we need is a taxi!"

Poor Rebecca's horrors continued. By most of today's standards the taxi driver was not a fast driver but to Rebecca and the children he was breaking the land speed record. At every corner, Rebecca shut her eyes and the children gripped ever harder. We went through some strange sights. Even the ice cream that Eva insisted that we buy for everyone did not reduce the panic they were feeling. They had never tasted anything so cold and sweet in their lives and like a lot of modern foods they are an acquired taste.

The taxi driver dropped us by St James' church and I paid him generously with some of the money Eva had 'earned'.

Of course it looked totally different now. The green grass that we had had our successful summer school on was now covered in houses. However the church was still there and to our amazement so was the house that once belonged to old Mrs Evans. Of course it didn't look the same. It had a conservatory for one thing and an extra floor and a double garage.

Rebecca was feeling a little more relaxed and she asked if she could take the children into the church. I assumed that this was either for sanctuary or to give prayer for surviving the journey she had just endured. Fortunately, the church was open, which is not the case with many inner city churches nowadays. She took Valentine from me and her two children followed her into the church.

The slight problem that faced us was, 'how do we get into the house to look for Margaret'?

As ever Eva had the answer. She went up and knocked on the door!

The lady who answered was obviously very busy and was in the process of dismissing Eva as some door-to-door evangelist or sales person, when Eva said, 'Can I show you something?"

This stopped the woman in her tracks. It was clear that she was a professional lady, perhaps having an office in the City which, although she worked at home, she visited from time to time.

"What do you want to show me?" she said abruptly.

"The lady who is stood behind you?" and as had happened so many times before, Eva touched her lightly on the arm and pointed behind her.

The lady hesitated for a moment, maybe thinking it was some kind of distraction by a cunning young thief, but then she turned slowly around to look at whatever Eva was pointing at. The experience of a person seeing a ghost for the first time was usually shock followed by fainting or a scream. Neither of these happened although I cannot imagine that the lady wasn't shocked.

Her reaction was quite calm in fact.

"You know I knew that there was something paranormal about this house from the moment I set foot in it. Who is she?"

"Can John and I come in and explain? We need to talk to Margaret."

"Is that her name?"

"Yes and I am Eva and this is John, my . . . . whatever!"

I'd gone from grandfather to father, back to grandfather and now whatever!

"I'm Carol."

In the conversation that followed it was revealed that Carol Wolstencroft was a hypnotist who dealt with people's emotional problems which ranged from trying to give up smoking to coping with phobias. She had done a bit of research into the paranormal while she was at university, hence the somewhat muted reaction to seeing her first ghost.

Eva briefly explained our predicament and it was met with total belief. She asked questions about the house at the time when Margaret was born and what the village was like in the early 17th century. Eva even explained that we had three visitors from that time who had taken sanctuary in the church.

"I will go and fetch them."

"Do you want some tea and a piece of cake?"

"Yes please, although I am not so sure what Rebecca and the children will make of hot tea."

I went outside and turned left and into the church yard. As I expected they were sat together in the front pews in prayer.

"Sorry." I said as I approached them, "We have met a lovely lady called Carol who lives in the house in which Margaret was born. She wants you to come in and have something to eat and drink."

Slightly reluctantly, they rose and followed me out of the church. All three seemed to be in a state of shock.

Rebecca was a bit unsure about the hot tea on such a warm day. I tried to convince her that it was the best drink when the weather was warm, but in truth I have never believed that myself. A cold beer always seemed a better bet.

Charlotte and Jacob enjoyed the chocolate cake but what the orange squash after it tasted like only they would know. They seemed to have calmed down since their abrupt entry into the 21st century and were not clinging on to their mother quite so tightly.

Carol was very understanding and not fearful of her strange visitors. She made them welcome. After the introductions and explanations were done, Eva apologized to Carol saying that unfortunately we had several things still to do.

It had become apparent that Rebecca and the children wanted to go home and by that they meant back to Southam in the 17th century. Rebecca and the children had made some good friends during our 'summer school' time and they thought that the village was an ideal place to live and work. Rebecca even had the idea of maybe opening up the school again. She had done well at her reading and writing lessons, and was intelligent enough to pass her knowledge on to others.

Eva excused herself so that she could have a few words with Margaret about her help in getting us back to the appropriate time. Carol asked if she too could talk with Margaret, through Eva of course.

I couldn't help noticing how Rebecca and the children were fascinated by all the trinkets that Carol had displayed around the house. Anne Stow's house had had a few, but Carol's was a veritable 'Aladdin's cave'.

"Homes are very much different in this time," Rebecca said.
"Yes they are. Because people can travel much more on cars, trains and airplanes, they tend to collect what we call ornaments from all over the world. Carol must be a much travelled lady. See those wooden faces? They are from Africa."

Charlotte's curiosity got the better of her and she spent some time looking closely at the teddy bears and colourful plates that adorned the surfaces.

"My wife collected 389 spoons from all the places we had visited and even friends brought spoons back for her from their travels."

"Even Hampton Court Palace doesn't have that many spoons."

Carol and Eva re-entered the room. Carol noticed that Charlotte and now Jacob were looking at her collection of teddy bears. She picked up two of them and offered them to Charlotte and Jacob. They looked at their mother for a sign and she nodded at them.

"You must both thank the lady."
They both did so profusely.

"Have we sorted something out with Margaret?"

"Yes. First I will take Rebecca, Charlotte and Jacob back to Southam in1605 and then we will return Valentine to his mother and job done."

"What about us going back to Castleford?"

"Oh yes, I hadn't thought of that but it should be no problem. We have done it once before and I still have some money left for a train or a taxi!"

The next few minutes were, for me, very sad. I had grown attached to Rebecca and her two lovely children. It was clear that Eva felt the same as tears began to roll down her cheeks.

"I am sure we will meet you two again at some time in the future," Rebecca said optimistically, "it has been the adventure of a lifetime and all three of us are thankful for all your kindness and love."

We kissed and hugged for several minutes but then it was time for them to leave and so using one of Margaret's 'corridors of transit' they departed with Eva for 1605.

That left Carol, Valentine and me all alone. The feeling was quite unusual.
"Thank you for all your understanding," I said to Carol to break the silence, "and the presents of the two bears."

"Do you think the little one would like a teddy bear too?"
"I am sure he would. It will be the only memento of his travels into another time."

He looked delighted with his gift.

"Will you do this again with Eva, travel in time I mean?"
"No definitely not. Too much danger and excitement for my liking. Eva might of course. She is the one with the special powers."
"She could become a medium, and get in touch with dearly departed relatives, for a price of course."
"She could but I think that would be far too mundane for Eva. I believe she liked the excitement of getting involved in the Gunpowder Plot."

At that moment, Eva arrived back. Her eyes were still red from crying.

"Are you OK?"

"Yes I think so. Let's get on with the other task of getting this young man back to his mother." She picked Valentine and teddy bear up and he giggled.

"What's this you have got? A teddy bear?"

To our amazement Valentine looked at the young girl and said "Evaaa"

This brought more tears and an extra special cuddle for Valentine.

"We must go."

We thanked Carol once again for all her understanding and Eva promised that she would return to visit her and Margaret. We left the room to find Margaret.

Apparently Eva had had a long conversation with Margaret about her mother Nancy and the day she was born. Surprisingly Margaret's mother had told her all about Eva who had come from another time but who would come back to see her.

Hopefully, for the penultimate time we entered that bright corridor belonging to the spirit world, and for the last time, I hoped, we entered the 17th century and more precisely the year of Margaret's death, 1645.

Valentine's return

It's strange when you land somewhere and you don't know where you are or what time of the year it is. All I knew is that we arrived at the time and place of Margaret's death. We had only Jon's word for where and when as Margaret was a bit vague on the matter. To be fair to her it was nearly four hundred years ago!

Jon had said 18th January 1645 and in the town of Bedford. If this was true we would have about ten miles left to do to get to Great Staughton. We had passed this way before in 1642 and it had been very dangerous. Gone was the relative calm of 1605, now we were in real danger in the Civil War. In 1642 we had swapped sides, depending on who confronted us. Then the battle was fairly even, now the tide had swung in favour of the Parliamentarians or the Roundheads, as the King's men had called them. Oliver Cromwell had put together what was to become known as the 'The New Model Army'. In 1644, somewhat against the odds, he had won the Battle of Marston Moor near York. This city had been a Royalist stronghold at the time.

I knew all this because sadly it was at this battle that Valentine's father, also called Valentine had died.

I didn't look too closely at Margaret as we transferred ourselves to 1645, but Eva had mentioned on arrival that the bullet that killed poor Margaret had left very little trace as it was a single shot through the heart. The kind of skirmishes that had brought Margaret's life to an end were common around the country at this time and we had encountered a number of them on our last visit.

Although we had done the journey from Bedford to Great Staughton once before, there were three main differences. Last time we had bought the horse Cropredy but this time we had no 17th century money so this was not an option. Sadly a taxi was not an option either.

Secondly, previously we had met a non-too-friendly ghost who in spite of this had been helpful in giving us accurate directions. Finding Susan would be a real benefit. She had been, at one time, engaged to the young Valentine who we had in our possession, before she died of consumption. This disease had reduced this once very pretty girl to a shadow of her former self. Sadly, she would not be around at this time in 1645.

Thirdly, it was January not October.

Our initial journey on this really cold day took us to the village of Broham and then on to Roothams Green. Despite the weather, for some reason, we were both now in no hurry to complete our mission. Nothing was said. Maybe a combination of carrying and walking with Valentine across fields and our realization that this hopefully was the end of a terrific adventure had given us a sense of anti-climax. There was still the explanation to Hester as to what had happened three years previously and whether she would believe that this child was her long-lost son. After all she must have thought that he died in that fire in 1642.

Our first problem started as we entered the village of Roothams Green. It started to snow, not just a few flakes but a blizzard. For the first time I could remember Valentine started to cry, I guess through him being very cold. Having come from a very hot day in 2008 or was it 2009, we were not clothed for a winter trek.

We found shelter in a barn. We were all cold and hungry and Eva and I were a bit annoyed with ourselves that we could have been so stupid as not to bring food and clothing from the 21st century. We were de-mob happy and not thinking ahead and poor Valentine was suffering. However we felt safe and putting Valentine between us we could use our body heat to give him a bit of comfort. It wasn't enough, he continued to cry. It is far easier to deal with your own illness than it is with that of others particularly when it was a young child who could not explain what was wrong. There was something very definitely wrong with him now.

"What do you think we ought to do now?" Eva asked.
"Not sure. There's something not quite right with Valentine."

"I have an idea. Maybe there is a friendly spirit around who could take us back to the 21ˢᵗ century and maybe get some medicine. He seems to be holding his tummy, so maybe some 'gripe water'. That's what Mum gave me and our Sophie when our stomachs were upset."

It was certainly a plan but we were not sure what had brought on Valentine's illness.

"You cuddle Valentine and I will go and search around a bit." With that she left the barn.

I tried my best to comfort poor Valentine. The light faded as night set in and by squeezing his stomach gently it seemed to give him some relief. I was beginning to worry because Eva hadn't returned after what seemed like an hour. Valentine, like most children, had found comfort in sucking his left thumb and was drifting in and out of sleep, with the occasional whimper.

Suddenly the relative calm was broken when Valentine was violently sick all over me. Maybe it was some kind of food poisoning and the rejection of the food was the body's way of dealing with this. A retching child is one of the more disconcerting sights and I felt powerless to help. After the retching was over, Valentine became hot and seemed to be sweating.

There was a noise from the barn door and an old woman entered, clearly no ghost. Behind her came Eva.

"My poor dear child!" the lady said.
"This is Mary," said Eva, "and she thinks she can help."
"He's just been sick and seems in a bad way."
"And this is her husband," Eva said touching my arm and pointing to the door.

The man was clearly in a bad way, not surprisingly since Eva had needed to touch me in order for me to see him, therefore he must be dead.

"I'll explain later," Eva said.

The lady took Valentine into her arms and seemed to be examining him, "Come with me into the house. I have a potion that may help the young child. He needs to be warmer."

We followed her out of the barn and into a neighbouring cottage. It was still snowing heavily and was already a few centimetres deep. The cottage was warm and cosy but the smell of smoke made it a little difficult to breathe.

Malcolm J. Brooks

"I've explained our predicament to her," Eva whispered, "and she thinks she can help us get to the Manor. She used to work there as a maid until she got too old."

"Does she know about her husband?"
"You mean about him being dead? Of course she does! I think that she is like me."
"What, a proper little madam?"
"No! She has the powers to see ghosts. I was really surprised that she could see and talk to her husband without my help and she was quite impressed that I could see and talk to him too."

"Can she travel through time?"
"I'm not sure. We never spoke about that. She is frightened to talk to people about her powers because she will be thought of as a witch and they might burn her to death or whatever they do to witches nowadays."

"She must be really pleased to see you!"
"She was and we had a long chat about what we could do."
"Do you thing that she can help poor Valentine?"
"Yes, I think so. She has travelled and seems to know a lot about modern medicine."

"How did her husband die?"
"Albert? He died three years ago at the Battle of Edgehill, fighting for the Royalists. That's another thing that Mary is not too keen to talk about. She is keeping her head down, so to speak."

"Your granddaughter says that you are from the future."
I was back to grandad! "Yes we are from the 21st century. Have you been there?"

She smiled. "No. I have never had the yearning to do such a thing even if my powers let me. I am happy seeing friends who have died and of course Albert."

"Have you always had the special powers that you have?"

"I first noticed them when I was a young child and they frightened me."

"That is exactly like Eva, except perhaps 'frightened' is not the correct word."

"She is a remarkable young woman, is she not?"

"Yes, she is, in more ways than one. Can you do anything to help poor Valentine?"

"Yes, I think so and I can take you both to the manor tomorrow and see Lady Walton."

"That would be excellent. Thank you. What do you think is wrong with Valentine?"

"I think I know what is wrong with him."

"What is it?"

"Eva said that you gave Valentine what she called an 'ice cream'. What is it made of?

"Milk and other things, all frozen together!" I said vaguely.

"Valentine will not have had such a thing before and his stomach is rejecting it. He is not used to such modern food, whatever it tastes like."

"A kind of colic?"

"I am not familiar with that term."

"Eva said that you had something that would help him."

"Yes, I have and hopefully by tomorrow he will feel better."

I didn't dare ask what it was; maybe some form of anti-acid medicine. We had to trust her and her knowledge of 17th century medicine.

———

We awoke to another very cold snowy day. Valentine's stomach seemed to have settled with whatever Mary had given him. However, he was sucking his thumb more than I had ever seen him do before.

Eva and I helped Mary to get her horse and very basic cart ready. It was nothing like the one that the men at Jon Stow's funeral had left behind and that had become our home for some weeks, but it was better than walking in all the snow that had fallen.

Albert was left to 'look after' Valentine, if a ghost can do such a thing. Valentine had gone back to sleep after his disturbed night and Albert was watching over him.

We had done a little bit of talking the previous night by firelight as the snow fell outside. It was quite magical really and took me back to 1963 the year my Nanna Eva died. The four of us swapped stories about the 21st and 17th centuries and the difference in living in them. Albert seemed to enjoy the company of people, other than his wife, who could see him and hear his reminiscences. He was intrigued to find out that we had been on that very hill where he had died at the Battle of Edgehill.

We set off on the relatively short journey to Great Staughton Manor with Mary at the reins and Eva cuddling an improving Valentine. We were all wrapped up in the rugs and blankets that Mary had provided. As she had worked at the Manor for some years she knew the shortest route well. There weren't many landmarks as far as I could remember from three years before but there were a couple. As we entered the village of Great Staughton, there was the familiar sight of a sundial erected in the centre of the village. We crossed a river the name of which I had forgotten and then passed a public house called the White Hart Inn, which was obviously a coaching station of some sort.

Eventually, the church belonging to Great Staughton came into view which meant that we had a mile to go. A mile to the end of a journey like no other. Eva looked at me.

"I am a bit sad really that soon it will all be over."
I smiled but was not sure I agreed, "We still have some work to do but being with Mary will help. I do not know how Hester will react."

The gate still showed the Walton coat of arms, a simple crest with a double upward arrow on it. The house was at the end of a long drive, and as we approached it we could see that it still had a double moat around it with a double bridge up to the main door. The house seemed to sit on an island.

Mary brought the horse to a stop in front of the snow-covered bridge.
"Here we are. Lady Walton may be out of course but someone will be in at the Manor and I still know quite a few of the servants who work here."

The last time Eva and I had knocked on the door of Great Staughton Manor, it had been opened by a large, rather unfriendly, gentleman known as Jeffries. Sadly it was he that caused the fire in which he died and resulted in us returning to 2006 with Valentine.

This time it was opened by a slim woman dressed in what looked to me like a servant's uniform.

"Hello Mary," came the warm response, "how are you? It is good to see you again."
"Hello Lucy. I am fine and how are you?

The initial greetings over, Mary introduced Eva and me but said nothing of the young child in my arms. She asked if we could see the lady of the manor and without hesitation, Lucy invited the four of us in.

The entrance hall had obviously been changed as a result of the fire in 1642, but the majestic stairs with their iron banisters were still a great feature.

"If you stay here I will get milady to come and talk to you."

Shortly after Hester and Lucy reappeared. Hester was now in her mid to late twenties and looked apprehensive. She seemed to look at Valentine and then turn away.

"We can talk in the reception room." We all crossed the hall and into the same reception room that we had been in three years earlier. Of course it was very different. This had been the seat of the fire and must have been totally gutted.

Before anybody else could speak Eva said, "It is all my fault Lady Walton! What I am about to tell you is true but you will not understand some of it."

"What do you mean, little girl." I think Hester was a bit taken aback by Eva's confession.

"Do you remember meeting John and me about three years ago just before the fire started?"
She looked at Eva and then at me and back to Eva. "Yes I do, but you both died in the fire along with my poor Valentine and our butler Jeffries." She looked agitated but addressed Mary. "What is the meaning of this visit?"

"It is so difficult for us to explain milady, but this child here is Valentine!"
"No, no. He is dead. He died in the fire," she screamed. "Is this some form of trick? What do you want of me?"

257

Eva tried again. "This is Valentine and I can prove it to you."

Hester looked aggressively at Eva. "Shut up child. You do not know what you are talking about."

Remarkably, Eva remained calm. "May I approach you Lady Walton?"

"What do you mean? Go away child. I want you all to leave me in peace."

I couldn't blame Hester for acting like this. For three years she had believed that her only son, and the only son she was likely to have, had died tragically in a house fire after two mysterious visitors had turned up unannounced.

"I want you to meet someone who will tell you all about what has happened to your son, Valentine."

I assumed that she was referring to either me or Mary. Eva walked towards Hester but she pulled away, not letting Eva touch her. I agree that what I did next has no protocol with ladies in the 17th century but it was the only thing I knew I could do.

It wasn't the perfect rugby tackle but as she wasn't expecting it, it was so easy to perform. I gently gave Valentine to Mary and suddenly sprang forward. I pushed Hester onto the long settee and held her down with my weight advantage.

Not unnaturally she screamed, loud and hard, and at any moment I was certain that a number of burly servants would come to her aid.

"Do it now," I shouted at Eva not knowing exactly what 'it' was. Eva moved forward swiftly and held Hester's shoulder. Hester screamed again even louder and then she collapsed into a faint. As anticipated a burly man did arrive at the door.

Quickly Mary said, "It's alright Rogers. Lady Walton just had a fright. She will be alright in a moment. Could you fetch a small glass of water for her?"
He hesitated and then turned to do as he was requested.

"I guess that you wanted to show her something?"

Valentine had started to cry again, what with all the noise going on and his current fragile state of health. Eva took her arm from Hester's shoulder and put it on mine, nodding her head towards the furthest wall. I stood up leaving Hester prone on the settee and looked in the direction that Eva had indicated.

There, with all his battle scarred body, stood Valentine Walton, husband of Hester and father of young Valentine. He was the man whose plight had touched Eva's heart and started the adventures we had had. For the first time in nearly three years I heard him speak.

Quietly and without emotion he said, "Thank you Eva for everything that you have done. Now please give me one more chance to speak to Hester, my dearest love."

Eva hesitated, "But Valentine you can remain here with Hester and your son for ever and see them every day if you wish."

He looked perplexed.

"Eva is correct," said Mary, "we have found that we have similar powers and with your permission I will happily come as often as you like to the Manor and be your way of communicating with your family."

Valentine smiled, which is something that he had never done in my presence before. He still looked grim from the injuries that he had sustained at the Battle of Marston Moor the year before, but the realization that he could still have some sort of relationship with his family had brought about a relieved look on his face which was really pleasing to see.

"Do you think Hester knows that Valentine is dead?"
"Yes," replied Mary, "the news came through some months ago."

"We need to give it one more go when Hester recovers, Eva, but more steadily this time."
"It was you that decided to do it the physical way!" she said, slightly hurt by my remark.

"OK point taken. Don't we need to put Hester's feet above her head?" I said, which probably wasn't the best way to put it, but I think Mary understood!

At that moment Rogers arrived with the water.

"Thank you, Rogers. That will be all for the moment," said Mary as she began the process of gently moving Hester's legs onto the edge of the settee, thus elevating them slightly.

Moments later a very groggy Hester stirred from her enforced position on the settee.
"What happened?"
"You fainted, milady," said Mary. "Please may I once again show you the same person that Eva showed you before you fainted?"

Hester looked fearful once again. "It is your husband, Valentine," said Eva pre-empting any further questions.

Her second look at her husband, this time with Mary's help, also brought a scream of shock but no fainting. She stared at her husband in disbelief.

"How can this be! Valentine is dead. He died in battle."
"Let Valentine explain," Mary replied in a calm voice.

The conversation that followed between Hester and Valentine was, for me, a one-sided dialogue. I wasn't in contact with anyone who could let me hear what Valentine was saying. I was quite content with this situation as I was pretty certain that I knew all the main details of what Valentine would be saying.

After about fifteen minutes of questions and answers, Hester's demeanour changed as she realized that some people were blessed with powers that could help her communicate with her husband. More importantly, she had back her son, whom she thought had been taken from her for ever.

It could not have been an easy time for Hester, but slowly and surely she came to terms with what had happened. Then on Hester's insistence we stayed at the Manor for one final night, this time with no fire to awaken us in the middle of the night.

———

With the saddest of farewells, particularly between Eva and Valentine Junior, we entered for the last time a 'corridor of transit'. It was fitting that the final transit was with the person who had started it all. The bright light encompassed us as we walked forward towards Valentine.

The next moment we were standing in bright sunshine in the middle of what seemed to be a building site. There were some men at work building walls around us. I don't know who was the more surprised, them or us.

"Where is the mission church?" said Eva.
"I don't know. This certainly isn't it."
"What are you two doing here?" a voice yelled.

"What has happened to St James' Mission Church?" I replied.

He looked a little perplexed. "It's been knocked down and we are building a bungalow here instead."
"Why?"
"Why what?"
"Why was the church knocked down?"
"Too expensive to run with so few people going to the services. It's really sad."
"This Mission Church was built for a community. It was a youth club, a dance hall and a social club as well as a church." I must have sounded angry.
"Sorry mate, but I am going to have to ask you to leave so we can get on with building the bungalow."

"Come on John. There's nothing we can do. Bye Valentine. Bye Nanna Eva."
"Is Nanna Eva with us?"
"She always is John. She always is. She's our guardian angel."

17th July 2048

Today would have been my hundredth birthday. Eva is fifty-three years old and has two children, unsurprisingly she called them Charlotte and Jacob. However, there is no evidence as yet that they have their mother's special powers. We still meet up regularly in Hampton Court when she brings her children down to London. Hampton Court was an ideal choice as a special place because Rebecca and her children are there. OK, the two queens can be a bit of a pain but things cannot be perfect all of the time.

With the St James' mission church gone, and a bungalow built in its place, I managed to buy the bungalow when it became available. Maybe I paid a little over the odds for it but it was well worth it and since I died there it is the place I meet Harry, Pearl (my parents) and of course Nanna Eva. Funny how things turn out!

My wife, Ann, did eventually forgive me for my 'running off' although it took the police and judicial authorities a little longer. The clincher with Ann was when Eva introduced her to Valentine's father one evening in the bungalow. She never wished to have the experience again but it proved that our incredible story had some truth.

Grace recovered but is still badly scarred. For her, the adventure did not go so well, and I felt sorry for her that she was inadvertently swept up in our adventure. To her credit she backed up my story, strange as it was, and the judge and jury had just enough doubt in their minds to acquit me of any wrong-doing. I don't think Eva did anything she shouldn't have done to sway the jury!

Grace never married and for that I feel responsible, since her burns had scarred her in more ways than one. She had to undergo lots of professional help as well as surgery.

Valentine appeared in my bungalow from time to time, but of course I was unable to see him while I was alive until I had a visit from Eva. His son went on to be a successful politician and played a big part in the 'Glorious Revolution' to remove King James II in 1688 and 1689. He died in 1716 in the reign of George I at the great old age of seventy-four. They meet, so Valentine Senior says, from time to time on the land that was once occupied by Great Staughton Manor. Sadly it was beset by yet another fire which burned it to the ground and it was never rebuilt.

I would guess that Valentine Junior had no memory of his two adventures with people from another time although there may just have been a vague memory of this amazing girl with whom he played strange games in his early years. The games may even have involved people from another world!

Rebecca too went on to live to a ripe old age but was one of the many victims of the 1666 plague. Charlotte went on to be a nurse for both sides in the Civil War whilst Jacob became a successful doctor. We did bring back all our Germolene and Elastoplasts since it would not have been fair to have robbed someone of two great inventions.

Eva visited me often while I was alive and living in the bungalow. She cannot visit the bungalow quite so easily now as it is owned by a young couple with two young daughters. She currently runs an antique shop in Castleford with her husband, so you can make up your own mind about how she gets her artifacts! I hope that she hasn't shown her powers to her lovely family, but maybe she does nip off now and then for a beer in the 17ᵗʰ century and to collect her antiques!

While I was alive we would celebrate Bonfire Night together with our families and remember that there are two sides to every story. We remembered John Wright, Jon Stow and of course Thomas Percy who in their different ways had an effect on our lives. Ann always showed an interest in what Eva and I recounted about the adventures but probably thought that I was exaggerating, as I often did.

Eva and I often talked about our two adventures and despite their problems we agreed that we would not have had it any other way. Very few people have the opportunity to travel back in time when they are alive.

I wonder what our attitude would have been if we had met somebody from the year 2408. What might those four hundred years bring in technological advances and which diseases would be cured? How would we have reacted to their advanced knowledge? Would everybody have Eva's special powers and so the world of the living and the dead become entwined? We would never know, well not for four hundred years.

There is, for certain, a lot more to learn about the world we live in and the Universe that surrounds us.

However, the one thing that Eva taught me is that everybody has some kind of special powers and that whatever fate throws at you, you must follow your dream and strive to be happy.

Lightning Source UK Ltd.
Milton Keynes UK
UKOW02f1136040914

238051UK00001B/24/P